'MISS READ'

VILLAGE
CENTENARY

Illustrated by J. S. Goodall

PENGUIN BOOKS

Penguin Books Ltd Harmondsworth, Middlesex, England
Penguin Books, 40 West 23rd Street, New York, New York 10010, U.S.A
Penguin Books Australia Ltd, Ringwood, Victoria, Australia
Penguin Books Canada Ltd, 2801 John Street, Markham, Ontario, Canada L3R 1B4
Penguin Books (N.Z.) Ltd, 182–190 Wairau Road, Auckland 10, New Zealand

First published by Michael Joseph Ltd 1980
Published in Penguin Books 1982
Reprinted 1982, 1984

Made and printed in Great Britain by
Richard Clay (The Chaucer Press) Ltd, Bungay, Suffolk
Set in VIP Garamond

900124477

TO
MARY AND VICTOR
WITH LOVE

Contents

1. *January*

It was Miss Clare who first pointed out that Fairacre School was one hundred years old.

It was a bleak Saturday afternoon, and we were enjoying hot buttered toast by the schoolhouse fire. Outside, the playground, and beyond that the fields and distant downs, gleamed dully white in the fading light. It had snowed every day since term started over a week ago, and from the look of the leaden skies, more was to come.

The leafless trees stood stark and black in the still air. Distant hedges smudged the whiteness, and a flock of homing rooks fluttered by like flakes of blackened paper.

It looked like a sketch in charcoal from the schoolhouse window. The only spot of colour in this black and white world came from the crimson glow of a bonfire in Mr Roberts's field next to the school. During the day the flames had leapt and danced while a haze of blue smoke wavered about them, but now that the men were homeward bound the fire was dying down – the one warm, glowing thing to be seen.

Indoors we were snug enough. Between us, in front of the log fire, stood the tea tray, the cups steaming fragrantly with China tea. The lamp glowed from the bookshelf behind Miss Clare's white head, making a halo of her silver hair. Miss Clare knows Fairacre School well, for she was both pupil and teacher there for many years, and was serving as infants' teacher when I was first appointed as headmistress, until ill health caused her retirement.

Since she was six years of age she has lived in a small cottage in the next village of Beech Green – a cottage

thatched by her father, and later by the young man who inherited her father's thatching tools. She lives alone in her old age. Her childhood friend, Emily Davis, shared the cottage with her until she died some time ago, and although Dolly Clare has adapted herself to solitary living with the courage and sweetness of disposition which has character- ized all her life, nevertheless, I know that at times she is lonely and appreciates a few hours in someone else's company.

I suspect that the winter is a particularly solitary time for her. In the summer, she busies herself in the cottage gar- den, or makes the jams and jellies for which she is renowned. Friends from neighbouring villages or from the market town of Caxley drive out to visit her, enjoying a country outing. There are more calls around Christmas, with visitors bearing gifts and good wishes. But after Christmas, with excitement past and dark evenings, icy roads, and the blight of winter ailments all taking their toll, the long dark nights hang heavily and I try to fetch Dolly occasionally to share my hearth and modest repast, and to give me the inestimable pleasure of her quiet and wise companionship.

'My mother used to say,' said Miss Clare, stirring her tea, 'that once January was over you could look forward to having a walk after tea in daylight.'

'That really is something to look forward to,' I agreed. 'Let's hope we get an early spring. The children haven't had one playtime outside yet, and they are all suffering from the January blues – a horrid disease.'

'It was always so. I expect the first headmistress said much the same thing a hundred years ago. By the way, are you proposing to celebrate the centenary?'

'To be honest, I hadn't realized we were a hundred until you pointed out the date over the door just now. I suppose we'll have to do something to mark such an occasion.'

'We had quite a bustle, I remember, when we were fifty years old in the thirties,' said Miss Clare. 'Mind you, it made a lot of talk. Some people wanted to take the children to London for the day. The Wembley Exhibition some years before had been a great success with the village people, all bowling up in charabancs, and having a marvellous time.'

'Did you go?'

'Indeed I did, and I think the statue of the dear Prince of Wales in butter was the thing that impressed me most!'

'Were there any other suggestions?'

'Oh, plenty! You know what village decisions are as well as I do. There were weeks of discussion – I was going to say *wrangling* – and dozens of ideas, but in the end we just celebrated with a marvellous tea party, and really everyone was happy.'

'I can see I shall have to start thinking about it. You'll have to let me know what some of those ideas were. One thing sparks off another when it comes to sharing suggestions.'

'No doubt you'll find some help in the log book,' said Miss Clare. 'There were lots of meetings held in the school, and I expect some of the decisions were recorded. And I'll certainly rack my brains for possible ideas. It will be fun to have something to look forward to.'

Her eyes sparkled at the thought, and I could not help feeling that my old friend was more enthusiastic about the village centenary than I was at the moment. No doubt though, I told myself bracingly, once I got down to it I should feel quite as excited about the celebration of our historic century as did my companion.

Later that evening I drove Miss Clare through white lanes to Beech Green. The roof of her cottage was topped with snow. The moon was rising and the sky was pricked with stars. Already the frost had formed, and we crunched our way up to the front door.

We made our farewells and before I returned to the car I turned to her. 'Let's make another date for the first of February,' I said. 'I'll fetch you after school, and we'll have that walk in daylight after tea, as your mother said.'

'That would be lovely,' agreed Miss Clare, and I left her at her door, the light from the cottage streaming out upon the winter garden, and our breath making little clouds before us as we waved farewell.

As so often happens when one's attention is drawn to something, references to the coming centenary came thick and fast.

Mr Willet, who is our school caretaker, church sexton, general odd job man for the village, producer of hundreds of plants for cottage gardens, as well as chief organizer of our village functions, raised the matter one slippery morning when I was approaching the school across the treacherous playground with considerable caution.

'What you needs,' said Mr Willet, holding out a horny hand to steady me, 'is a stout pair of socks over your shoes. No need to teeter along like a cat on hot bricks if you've got summat to foil the ice. Socks is the answer. It's a good tip, miss.'

I promised to remember.

'We doin' anything about us bein' a hundred this year?' he asked.

'I expect so.'

'Well, it ought to be done proper. Stands to reason, us should have a fitting sort of celebration. A hundred's a hundred. Fairacre'll expect summat good.'

I said that I would start thinking about it, and passed through the school door, almost colliding with Mrs Pringle who was advancing with a large wastepaper basket clutched to her cardigan.

Mrs Pringle is our school cleaner, a martyr to unspecified ailments in her leg, particularly severe when asked to undertake extra work, and a thorn in my flesh. While it is always a pleasure to encounter Mr Willet, to come face to face with Mrs Pringle calls for courage, patience and a bridling of one's tongue. Quite often, when my patience is exhausted, as Herr Hitler was wont to say, we have a sharp argument. Mrs Pringle is invariably the victor in these combats as she is quicker-witted, better-prepared and, I like to think, more intrinsically malevolent than I am.

However, she is an excellent worker, and if one can turn a deaf ear to the accompanying grumbles the results of her labours are splendid. I doubt if any other school in the county has such jet-black tortoise stoves, burnished to a satin finish with blacklead and elbow grease. Woe betide any child who is foolhardy enough to sully their perfection, particularly when they have been 'done up for the summer'. In that term, no matter how low the mercury in the thermometer drops, the stoves remain inviolate, and instead we don our cardigans philosophically.

Once a week she switches her attention to my house across the playground. I can't think that I am really much more slatternly than the majority of working women, but Mrs Pringle soon makes me think so. The odd crumb on the carpet, the splash of grease on the kitchen stove, or a day's dust on the mantelpiece, are seen instantly by Mrs Pringle's eagle eye and magnified tenfold. The day that she discovered a small crust of mouldy bread '*behind*, not even *in* the bread bin' was a red-letter day for the lady, and I have never been allowed to forget it. When Mrs Pringle tells me that she intends 'to bottom the sitting room', I make hasty plans to be away from home for the allotted time. I prefer to be absent when she finds the assorted objects which have hidden themselves at the sides of the armchair cushions. Life is quite complicated enough for a village schoolmistress without seeking further confrontations.

On this particular occasion, Mrs Pringle put the wastepaper basket on the floor and supported herself on her upturned broom. She looked a little like Britannia with her trident, but less elegant.

'Mr Willet tells me there's a lot of talk about us getting to the century. What, if anything, are we doing about it?'

'Oh, something, I hope,' I said airily. 'But of course it will need some thought. I shall have to have a word with the vicar, and the managers. And Miss Briggs,' I added, as an afterthought.

'Humph!' grunted Mrs Pringle. 'A fat lot of use *she'll* be!'

I was inclined to agree, but could not countenance our school cleaner criticizing my new infants' teacher, straight from college and trailing clouds of educational theories which were enough to curdle one's blood. She had only been with me since the beginning of term, and I sincerely hoped that she would soon settle down and do a little plain teaching instead of what she was pleased to call 'pastoral counselling'.

I decided to ignore Mrs Pringle's interjection, and changed the subject.

'There doesn't seem to be much soap in the wash basins, Mrs Pringle.'

'And whose fault's that?' demanded the lady. 'There was four pieces put out by my own hands when school started, and if them children is allowed to leave it wasting in the water, that's not my affair.'

She picked up the wastepaper basket and made towards

the door, where she turned to face me, her three chins wobbling fiercely.

'I'm not made of soap!' she declared, having the last word as usual, and vanished.

The weather continued to be abominable, with icy roads, fresh snowfalls and great difficulty in getting about.

Nevertheless, on my few visits within sliding distance in the village, I had been questioned by Mr Lamb of Fairacre Post Office, our vicar Gerald Partridge, Henry Mawne our local ornithologist, and a number of parents about the possibility of celebrating the school's centenary.

I took evasive action on all occasions. With the weather

as it was, there was quite enough to do keeping warm
oneself and seeing that the children, the school building
and one's own house were protected as much as possible
from the devastating cold. Time enough to think about the
centenary when the temperature rose, I decided. However,
I did consider one or two ideas as I sat close to my fire in the
evenings, my feet on the fender courting chilblains.

What about a concert? With songs, or music from each
of the ten decades? The fact that the Fairacre children are
not particularly musical, and that I am the only one who
can attempt to play the piano – preferably compositions
cast in the key of C – and that the audience was equally
limited in musical knowledge, seemed to make that idea a
non-starter.

Or a pageant? It could be based on the log book, with
various scenes. But then there were costumes to devise, and
we had no stage, and the thought of putting it on in the
playground made me realize the many hazards to be faced.
Or a display in the school of its hundred years of history? I
suppose one could collect photographs, and even a few old
exercise and text books, and the children could have theirs
on show, as on open days at the school.

I began to think that Miss Clare's recollection of the fifty
years' celebration had much to commend it. A mammoth
tea party sounded much more festive than my own doubt-
ridden ideas. But surely we could do better than that?

Certainly, Miss Clare had fairly sparkled with enthusiasm when she remembered the trip to Wembley and
the sight of the Prince of Wales, unforgettable in butter.
What about an outing? One of the historic houses within
fifty miles of Fairacre, perhaps? But we could do that at
any time, and outings were no great treat these days when
most parents owned a car. Besides, it seemed silly to go
away for a centenary celebration. The whole point of
celebrating a hundred years of Fairacre School's progress

was surely to have the occasion at the school, by the school, and for the pupils of that school, both past and present.

At that point in my mental meanderings I noticed that the fire needed more fuel, the coal scuttle was empty, and the log basket in the same sad condition. The clock said twenty to ten. Quite late enough for Fairacre folk to be up!

I put up the fireguard, looked out of the front door at the frosty world, and went thankfully to bed.

Miss Briggs, as Mrs Pringle had forecast, was not much help. Since Miss Clare's departure some years ago, I have had a number of infants' teachers, most of them young and very good company.

In a tiny school like ours, with only two teachers, it is essential that the staff is compatible. In most cases we have enjoyed each other's company, although a certain Miss Jackson, some years ago, was a sore trial, not only as a member of staff, but by being so silly as to fall headlong in love with the local gamekeeper, in the best tradition of D. H. Lawrence, and so worrying us all to death.

Miss Briggs had left college in the summer before, had been unable to obtain a post at the beginning of the school year in September, but arrived at Fairacre to take up her appointment in January. Her predecessor, a cheerful young married woman who had driven from Caxley each day, was starting a family, and I could only be grateful for the year of hard work and good company the school and I had enjoyed during that time.

For the first few days Miss Briggs had little to say to me but quite a lot, and in a loud hectoring tone, to her charges. The result was a noisy class, but I decided to bide my time before I interfered. The girl must find her feet, and I knew that a certain amount of noise – 'a busy hum', as college lecturers like to call it – was looked upon as downright beneficial these days. I am all for 'a busy hum' if it can be halted whenever the teacher so desires, but too often, I notice, that is not possible.

Then she was unduly anxious to leave school at three-thirty, when the infants were sent home. Those with older brothers and sisters usually waited the extra fifteen minutes until my class was free, and in the normal way, the infants' teacher was clearing up her classroom, or buttoning children into garments, in that quarter of an hour.

On several occasions I had seen her car drive away smartly at 3.31, and found a little knot of restless infants at large in their classroom awaiting the release of their kinsfolk in my room. Twice, parents had risked the icy roads to speak to her about some particular problem after school, but the lady had vanished, and I had to pass on their messages.

Clearly, I should have to speak to the girl before many days passed, and I did not relish it. I was fast coming to the conclusion that she was quite without humour, taciturn – perhaps a sulker when crossed – and decidedly lazy. On the whole, I like young people, and had been lucky with many vivacious and enthusiastic teachers in their first job with me. It seemed sad that I could strike no answering spark from Miss Briggs. 'A fair old lump of a girl,' Mr Willet had opined, three days after her arrival.

I was beginning to think that it just about summed her up.

Towards the end of the month, I began to wonder if a new skylight might be the best way of celebrating Fairacre School's hundredth birthday. For all that time, it seems, the skylight, strategically placed over the obvious site for the headteacher's desk, has let in rain, snow, wind, and the rays of the sun.

Throughout the pages of the log books mention of the skylight crops up:

'A torrential storm this afternoon delayed the pupils' departure from school, and precipitated a deluge through the skylight, damaging some of the children's copybooks and the Holy Bible.' So runs one entry in 1894.

Four years later we read the following somewhat querulous entry:

'Was obliged to shift my desk, as a severe draught from the skylight had resulted in a stiff neck and earache, both occasioning great pain.'

Hardly a year goes by without reference to new glazing or new woodwork needed by this wretched window. Nothing seems to improve it, and I can vouch for the beastly draught which had dogged all the headteachers, and the diabolical way it lets in water.

Mr Willet takes it all very philosophically and quotes irritatingly 'that what can't be cured must be endured'. The wind had been in the north-east, and I was in a more militant mood. If I have complained once about the skylight, during my term of office, I must have complained twenty times. The result has been some sympathy, a little tinkering, and not a jot of difference in improvement.

After three days of howling draught and wearing a silk scarf round my neck, I sat down to write to the office even more forthrightly than usual about my afflictions. On reading it through I was quite impressed with my firmness of tone, which was tempered with a little pathetic martyrdom, and which surely should bring results. I added a postscript about our hundred years at the mercy of this malevolence overhead, and hoped that something could be done permanently. Cunningly, I pointed out what a drain

on the county's economy this must have been over the past
century. Every little helps when pleading one's cause.

I posted my letter, wondering if it was a waste of a
stamp. Time would tell. On the way back, picking my
steps through the slushy snow which was taking its time to
disappear, I met Henry Mawne, our eminent ornithologist, who has been a good friend to all in the village.

'How's Simon?' was my first question. His young god-
son had attended my school for a short time, but his brief
stay was ended when a rare albino robin, the pride of the
village, came to a sudden death at the boy's hands.

'Settling down well at his prep school,' said Henry, 'and
I may as well tell you now, before you hear it on the
grapevine, that his father and Irene Umbleditch are getting
married.'

'I am delighted to hear it,' I said warmly. 'He's had so
much unhappiness, and he couldn't have anyone nicer than
Irene. What's more, Simon is so fond of her too.'

'Well, we're all mightily pleased about it,' said Henry.
'No doubt they'll be visiting us before long, and I hope you
will come and see them. They've never forgotten how
much you did for Simon. And for us,' he added.

We parted, and I returned home much cheered by this
good news. David's first wife had been afflicted by mental
illness and eventually had taken her own life. It was time
that he and poor young Simon had some sunshine, after the
shades of misery which they had suffered.

When I entered my house I found a fat mouse corpse on
the hearth rug, and Tibby sitting beside it looking particularly smug. Far from being praised, she was roundly cursed
as I put on my wellingtons again, collected the corpse by
the tail, and ploughed my way, shuddering, to the bound-
ary hedge and flung the poor thing into Mr Roberts's field.

I often wonder if he notices a particularly fertile patch
within a stone's throw of the schoolhouse garden. It is

nourished by a steady flow of Tibby's victims, and must
have made a substantial difference to his crops over the
years.

Like most people in Fairacre, my pupils enjoyed feeding
the birds during the winter, and our school bird-table was
always well supplied with bread, peanuts and fat.

As well as these more usual offerings, Mrs Pringle
supplied mealworms which the robins adored. She had first
undertaken this chore when our famous albino robin
appeared on the scene. After his death, in the grievous state
of mourning which followed, the supply of mealworms
ceased, but to our delight a second albino, probably a
grandchild of the first, was seen, and the mealworms were
hastily added to the menu.

Not that we saw a great deal of the second white robin. It
was obviously less bold than its predecessor, and more
cautious in its approach to the food we put out. As Henry
Mawne had warned us, the robins and other birds of
normal colouring would tend to harass the albino. It certainly seemed timid, but was all the more adored by the
children on that account. The first robin had frequently
come to the jar of mealworms during the day. The second
one only came occasionally, and there were days when it
did not appear at all.

One afternoon the children were busy making what they
term 'bird pudden', which consists of melted dripping
mixed with porridge oats, chopped peanuts and some cur-
rants. We had melted the fat in an old saucepan on the
tortoise stove, and I kept a weather eye on the door in case
Mrs Pringle should walk in unexpectedly and catch us
violating her beloved stove.

There was a comfortable smell of cooking in the classroom as Patrick stirred the ingredients with my wooden
jam-making spoon. The saucepan by now was on the floor.

Nevertheless, when the door opened, I nearly jumped out of my skin with guilt.

Luckily it was only the vicar.

'I seem to have startled you,' said the Reverend Gerald Partridge. 'I suppose I should have knocked.'

'Not at all. I just thought you were Mrs Pringle.'

'*Mrs Pringle*?' echoed the vicar. A look of the utmost perplexity distorted his chubby face. 'Now why on earth should you think that?'

'I'll tell you later,' I said hastily. 'Can I help you?'

The vicar put the plastic bag he had been carrying on my desk.

'A friend of mine who is in the publishing business has most kindly given me some children's books. I think he said he was *remaindering* them – a term I had not heard before, I must confess. Anyway, I thought they might go on the library shelf here.'

'Oh, splendid! We can always do with more books.'

He began to haul them out of the bag which bore the interesting slogan: *Come to Clarissa's For Countless Cosmetics*. It seemed an odd receptacle for a vicar to have acquired.

'I have looked them through,' he said earnestly, 'and they seem quite suitable. Really, these days, one can find the most unnecessarily explicit descriptions of deeds of violence, or of biological matters too advanced for our young children here.'

'I am sure your friend wouldn't give you anything like that,' I said reassuringly, 'but I will read them first if you like.'

'It might be as well,' said the vicar. He suddenly became aware of Patrick's activities.

'Whatever is the boy making?'

I explained, the children joining in with considerable gusto.

'Well, I heartily approve,' he said, when he could make himself heard. 'We must do all we can to keep the birds healthy and strong during this bitter weather.'

He began to walk to the door and I accompanied him. He spoke in a low voice.

'Are you sure that mixture is all right? It looks most indigestible to me.'

'The birds lap it up,' I told him. 'They've been doing so for months now so don't worry.'

He smiled and departed. I had barely returned to the stove preparatory to clearing away any mess before Mrs Pringle caught us, when the vicar reappeared again.

'I forgot to give you a message from my wife. Could you come to the vicarage for a drink on Friday at six-thirty? A few people are coming to discuss the arrangements for the Caxley Spring Festival.'

'Thank you. Yes, please, I should love to come,' I said.

He said goodbye for the second time and we set about the stove with guilty speed. Mrs Pringle's name had not been mentioned by anyone in the classroom, but we all knew what lent energy to our efforts.

That evening my old friend Amy rang me. We first met at college, many years ago, and the friendship has survived separation, a war, Amy's marriage and the considerable differences in our views and temperaments.

Amy is all the things I should like to be – elegant, charming, good-looking, intelligent, rich and much travelled. I can truthfully say that I do not envy her married state, for I am perfectly content with my single one, and in any case James, although a witty and attractive man, is hopelessly susceptible and seems to fall in love at the drop of a hat, which Amy must find tiresome, to say the least of it.

'Come and have some supper,' I invited when she proposed to visit me one evening in the near future.

'Love to, but I must warn you that I'm slimming.'

'Not *again*!' I exclaimed.

'That would have been better left unsaid.'

'Sorry! But honestly, Amy, you are as thin as a rail now. Why bother?'

'My scales which, like the camera, never lie, tell me that I have put on three-quarters of a stone since November.'

'I can't believe it.'

'It's true though. So don't offer me all those lovely things on toast that you usually do. Bread is *out*.'

'What else?'

'Oh, the usual, you know. Starch, sugar, fat, alcohol, and the rest.'

'Is there anything left?'

Amy giggled.

'Well, lettuce is a real treat, and occasionally a *small* orange, and I can have eggs and fish and lean meat, in moderation.'

'The whole thing sounds too damn moderate for me. What would you say to pork chops, roast potatoes and cauliflower with white sauce, followed by chocolate mousse and cream?'

'Don't be disgusting!' said Amy. 'I'm drooling already, but a nice slice of Ryvita and half an apple would be just the thing.'

'I'll join you in the pauper's repast,' I promised nobly, and rang off.

2. February

I remembered my promise to Miss Clare and brought her over to tea on the first of the month.

A gentle thaw had set in and the snow had almost vanished. It tended to turn foggy at night and the roads were still filthy, with little rivulets running at the sides, but it was good to have milder weather during the daytime, and a great relief to let the children run in the playground at break. Under the garden hedge a few brave snowdrops showed. I had picked a bunch for the tea table, the purity of the white flowers contrasting with the dark mottled leaves of the ivy with which I had encircled them.

I was glad that I was not slimming like poor Amy, as we munched our way through anchovy toast and sponge cake. After school I am always ravenous, and how people can bear to go without afternoon tea, and all the delightful ingredients which make it so pleasant, I do not understand.

When we had cleared away, we set out on the first after-tea walk of the year. A few early celandines showed their shield-shaped leaves on the banks at the side of the lane, and it was wonderful to see the green grass again after weeks of depressing whiteness.

A lark sang bravely above, and blackbirds and thrushes fluttered among the bare hedges, scattering the pollen from the hazel catkins that nodded in the light breeze. In the paddock near Mr Roberts's farmhouse, sixty or seventy ewes, heavily in lamb, grazed ponderously upon the newly disclosed grass. There was a wonderful feeling of new life in the air despite the naked trees, the bare ploughed fields and the miry lane we walked.

'I know most people dislike the month of February,' said Miss Clare, as we returned, 'but I always welcome it. With the shortest day well behind us, and the first whiff of spring about, I begin to feel hopeful again.'

'Your mother was quite right,' I told her. 'Everyone should have an after-tea walk on February the first. It's the finest antidote to the January blues I've come across.'

Dolly Clare laughed, and slipped her frail arm through mine. It was sharply borne in upon me how light and thin she had become during the last few years. Her bones must be as brittle as a bird's. Would my old friend survive to see the next spring? Would we share another first-of-February celebratory walk?

I hoped with all my heart that we might.

On the following Friday, I dutifully made my way to the vicarage. I had not heard any more about the Caxley Spring Festival which the vicar had mentioned, and wondered exactly how our small downland village, some miles from the market town, would become involved.

There were about twenty people in the Partridges' drawing room, and only two were strangers to me. Diana Hale, wife of a retired schoolmaster, was there. Their house, Tyler's Row, once four shabby cottages, is one of the show places of our village, and she and her husband are tireless in their good works.

I was pleasantly surprised, too, to see Miriam Quinn who came to live in Fairacre a few years ago. She is a most efficient secretary to a businessman in Caxley, likes a quiet life, and is somewhat reserved.

Like most newcomers to a village, I know that Miss Quinn was approached by most of the village organizations when she first took up residence at Holly Lodge on the outskirts of Fairacre, for her qualities of hard work and intelligence had gone before her and everyone said, as I find to my cost as a spinster, that a single woman must have time on her hands and enjoy a nice bit of company. Holly Lodge is the home of Joan Benson, a sprightly widow, and she and her lodger seem very happy together. Joan was not at the meeting, and I wondered how it was that Miriam Quinn had been coralled with the rest of us.

It was soon made clear. The vicar, who was acting as chairman, introduced the two strangers as the organizers of the Festival in Caxley, and Miss Quinn as Fairacre's representative.

We all sat back, sherry in hand, to listen obediently.

The Arts in Caxley, one of the strangers told us with some severity, were sadly neglected, and the proposed Festival was to bring them to the notice of Caxley's citizens and those who lived nearby. Let him add, he said (and who were we to stop him?), that he was not accusing Caxley people of *Philistinism* or *Cruelty to Creative Artists*, but merely of *Ignorance* and *Apathy*.

There was a great fund of natural talent in Caxley – and its surrounds, he put in hastily – and there would be two plays by local playwrights put on at the Corn Exchange, several concerts at the parish church, and exhibitions of painting, embroidery and other crafts at various large buildings in the town, and outside.

'What happens to the money?' Mr Roberts, our local farmer, asked bluntly. Farmers are noted for their realistic approach to life, and ours is no exception.

The speaker looked a little surprised by the interjection of such a materialistic inquiry in the midst of his eulogy about Caxley's artistic aspirations, but rallied bravely.

'I was just coming to that. Any profits will go to three local charities so that a great many people will benefit. They are named in the leaflets which we are distributing at this meeting.'

Mr Roberts grunted in acknowledgement, and the speaker resumed his talk. Miriam Quinn's involvement was then revealed, and she gave a sensible description of her part in the Festival.

'I'm really here to get suggestions,' she said. 'One way of helping, particularly for us in the country, is by opening our gardens. The vicar has already offered to have his open, and so has Mr Mawne. We can arrange a date to suit us all, and in May, when the Festival takes place, our gardens here are at their best.'

'What about the schoolchildren having a maypole? Dancing and singing and all that?' called out someone, well hidden from me.

Miriam Quinn looked at me hopefully.

'I'll think about it,' I said circumspectly. What with the centenary, and the skylight waiting to be repaired, I had some reservations about a May Day celebration as well.

'Beech Green had a street fair once,' said somebody.

'And only once,' said her neighbour. 'The traffic was something awful when Mr Miller's tractor broke down where the road narrows.'

The vicar, adept at handling situations like this, suggested that any ideas might be given to Miss Quinn at the end of the meeting. He was quite sure, he added, that she would receive every possible support from Fairacre in the part that the village would play in this excellent enterprise.

Were there any more questions?

At this, as always, silence fell upon the gathering. Sherry glasses were refilled, the guests circulated again, and we all knew, as we chattered of everything under the sun bar the matter in hand, that the Caxley Spring Festival would get plenty of attention once the meeting had dispersed.

*

Amy paid her visit to me one evening when the wind was scouring the downs, whistling through keyholes and making the schoolhouse shudder beneath its onslaughts.

Out in the garden the bare branches tossed up and down, and dead leaves flurried hither and thither across the grass. Overhead the rooks had battled their way home at dusk, finding it difficult to keep on course.

But my fire burned brightly in the roaring draught and Tibby, on her back, presented her stomach to the warmth, paws above her head. We were pretty snug within, whatever the weather did outside.

Amy arrived in a new suede coat of dark brown and some elegant shoes that I had not seen before. She held a bowl of pink hyacinths in her hands.

'Coals to Newcastle, I expect. I know you do well with bulbs.'

'Not a bit of it! Mine are over, and you couldn't have brought anything more welcome, Amy dear. Come in, out of this vile wind.'

She divested herself of the beautiful coat, and exclaimed with pleasure at the fire.

'I've been trying to do without one. After all, the central heating should really be enough – heaven knows it costs a small fortune to run – but there's something rather *soulless* about the electric fire which I'm forced to put on for an hour or two, now and then.'

'Well, you know me, Amy. I light a fire at the drop of a hat. I can always console myself with the thought that I have no central heating to make me feel guilty.'

'I've felt the cold far more this winter,' said Amy, stroking Tibby's stomach. 'Whether it's *anno domini* or just this slimming business, I can't tell. A bit of each, I expect.'

'How's the poundage going?'

'Much too slowly. If only I habitually drank gallons of

beer, or ate pounds of chocolate, I should find it quite easy to cut down the calories, but I eat like a bird.'

'Not worms, I hope.'

'Don't be facetious, dear. You know what I mean. I'm heartily sick of salad and cold meat.'

'Well, that's what you've got tonight. Unless you'd rather have a boiled egg.'

'Either would be delicious,' said Amy, lying bravely. 'Do you know, as a child, I refused to eat salad, particularly tomatoes.'

'My *bête noire* was beetroot,' I recalled. 'Now I love it, and coffee. I didn't touch it until we went to college. I'm sure tastes change as one goes through life.'

'They certainly do. But perhaps it's simply our aging digestive systems, do you think? I used to adore potted shrimps, but these days they go down like greased nails, and I have terrible indigestion.'

'We could have a nice bowl of thin gruel on our laps here,' I remarked, 'if you feel in such an advanced state of decay.'

'Not likely!' said Amy. 'Besides, gruel is fattening.'

'Who was it said that anything one enjoys turns out to be fattening or immoral?'

'No idea, but he knew what he was talking about,' said Amy with feeling.

Over our frugal repast, the conversation turned to Caxley's Festival. I told Amy about Miss Quinn's part in it and our dearth of suggestions in Fairacre.

'Well, in an expansive moment I agreed to have a poetry reading in my house. Do you think anyone will come?'

'The poets will, presumably.'

'That's what I'm afraid of. I mean, shall I be stuck with half a dozen sensitive types, possibly all jealous of each other and with no audience to listen to them? How can I be sure we get a nice, kind, attentive crowd?'

'They'll come,' I assured her. 'Lots of people will simply come to see your house and garden, poets or no poets. Others will be culture-vultures, and game to listen to anything in the cause of Art, and others will feel they can't waste the ticket.'

'And there are bound to be the poets' relations,' agreed Amy, looking more hopeful. 'I wonder if we could organize a group from the evening classes in Caxley? You know the sort doing English Literature? The Beowulf bunch, for instance.'

'"Weave we the warp. The woof is wub" sort of thing, you mean? I don't see why not. English Literature classes should swell the audience nicely, and if you're short, I'll come and sit in the front row.'

'I'm counting on you, anyway,' said Amy, selecting a large stick of celery, 'to pass round the sausage rolls.'

'You'll need something far more spiritual than sausage rolls,' I told her. 'You'll have to have nectar and ambrosia, and lots of "beaded bubbles winking at the brim" for a poetry evening.'

'We'll have lashings of the latter,' promised Amy, and crunched into the celery.

It was still blowing a gale when Amy left me at about nine-thirty. I saw by the light of her headlamps that a sizable branch had been torn from the horse chestnut tree in the garden, and the path was strewn with twigs and dead leaves. It was going to be pretty draughty sitting under that skylight tomorrow, I thought, if this weather continued.

I sat down by the fire again, and had a belated look at the daily papers. It was the usual conglomeration of strike threats, travel delays, violence, war and sudden death, and the most peaceful reading was the crossword and the obituaries.

The wind howled like a banshee and I found it distinctly unnerving. With Amy for company I had not noticed the vicious elements outside. Now, alone and responsible for any damage done, I became unusually jittery.

A cupboard door by the fireplace creaked slowly open, and I felt my blood pressure rising. Would a yellow claw-like hand with immensely long nails, Chinese fashion, appear round it? Or a black hand perhaps, holding a dagger? Or a white one dangling a knuckle duster?

'You've been reading too many bloods,' I thought, and steeled myself to shut the door firmly. At the same moment, Tibby rose, fur bristling, and advanced towards the kitchen door, growling horribly. I watched her, mesmerized. Could someone have broken in? Had I locked the back door earlier? Probably not, we are a trusting lot in Fairacre, and, under cover of the appalling racket outside it would be quite easy for someone to gain entry.

What should I do? Should I ring Caxley police? Should I arm myself with the poker and fight it out? Reason told me that any burglar, no matter how puny, could easily twist a weapon out of my grasp and use it to belabour me.

Surely I had read somewhere that it was best to offer no resistance. After all, hospitals are severely overcrowded without unnecessary casualties awaiting admission. If it were money that the intruder wanted he was going to be unlucky. I might rustle up three pounds or so, but that would be the most I could find in the schoolhouse at short notice. True, Aunt Clara's seed pearls might be acceptable, but that would constitute the bulk of my jewellery.

I took a deep breath, and flung open the door. The kitchen was as quiet as the grave. Tibby sat down and began to wash her face in the most maddeningly unconcerned fashion.

'Time I was in bed,' I told her, and went.

*

To my surprise, I had a letter from the office about the skylight. Obviously my pleas had touched some compassionate heart, and the gist of the reply was that this particular item, under 'minor works', would be treated as an emergency, and that Mr Reginald Thorn, of the Nook, Beech Green, had been instructed to call and examine the offending structure.

'Should have thought the office could've found someone with a bit more up top than old Reg,' commented Mr Willet, when I imparted the good news. 'Proper dog's dinner he'll make of it. I reckon I'd make a better job of it meself.'

I too had no doubts on that score, for Mr Willet's handiwork, whether with seedlings, paintbrush or bolts and screws, is always beautifully done. But the office had appointed Reg Thorn and that was that.

'When do you think he'll come?'

Mr Willet pushed back his cap to scratch his head.

'Now that's asking! I know for a fac' he's making a dresser for that new chap at Beech Green post office, and Mrs Mawne is going up the wall about some shelving he promised her last autumn and hasn't never done yet.'

'He's like that, is he?'

Mr Willett pursed his mouth judicially.

'Well, he's not a bad sort of chap, old Reg, but he's no flier. I mean, he *says* he'll do summat, and he means it too, but his trouble is he can't say "No" to no one, so the work sort of piles up.'

'So you reckon it'll be the summer before he gets round to our skylight?'

'Now, I'm not saying that. This bein' an office job like, and with forms and that to fill in, well, it might make old Reg get a move on. On the other hand, if all the other people get a bit whacky, and bully him, maybe he'll do their jobs to keep 'em happy. There's no telling.'

He raised his voice to a bull-like roar.

'Get off that there coke, you young devils, or I'll tan the skin off of your backsides, and you can tell your mums and dads why I done it!'

Mr Willet's method of dealing with the young might not find favour with modern psychologists, but it clears the coke pile in record time.

Whether Reg Thorn was awed by the county's official letter, or simply wished for a change of job, thus evading his earlier customers who were breathing fire, no one will ever know. But the outcome was decidedly cheering for me. Reg Thorn arrived within the week just as we were dishing out minced lamb (alleged – I suspected some man-made fibre) and mashed swede.

He was a tall lantern-jawed fellow, and said very little. He gazed up at the skylight with an expression of gloom. I had served all the children, and dispatched the containers to the lobby to await Mrs Pringle's ministrations, before he spoke.

'Rotted,' he said.

I agreed.

He sighed heavily.

'Still leaks?'

'It's been doing it for nearly a hundred years.'

'Ah! Looks like it.'

He remained rooted to the spot, very much in the way of the children returning their plates, but I did not like to say so. At length, he spoke again.

'Best see outside. All right?'

'Yes indeed. Mr Willet's ladder is by the wall if you want it.'

'Got me own. Insurance, see.'

To my relief he vanished, only to reappear framed in the skylight some minutes later. He appeared to be gouging pieces of wood from the window frame, and I only hoped that this operation would not add to the draught trouble.

I served helpings of crimson jelly decorated with blobs of rather nasty artificial cream. It is the children's favourite sweet and I was kept so busy scraping the tin for second helpings that I was quite startled to see Reg again at my elbow.

'Needs a dormer,' he shouted above the clatter.

'Won't that be expensive?'

'Yes.'

'Well, it's up to the people at the office,' I shouted back. 'You can only tell them what you think.'

'Ah!' agreed Reg, and plodded off towards the door.

'My mum,' said Patrick conversationally, 'says old Reg don't get nothin' done in a month of Sundays.'

'That will do,' I replied witheringly. Privately, I feared that Patrick's mum was probably dead right.

Time alone would tell.

There is a widespread belief among town dwellers that remarkably little happens in the country. As any villager will tell you, the amount of activity that goes on is quite exhausting.

I am not thinking of the agricultural pursuits by which most of us get our living, but of the social side of life. What with the Women's Institute, amateur dramatics, various regular church activities such as choir practice and arranging the flowers, Cubs and Brownies for the younger people, fêtes, jumble sales and whist drives, one could be out every night of the week if one so wished.

As village schoolmistress I try not to take on too much during term time, although I do my best to make amends in the holidays, but nevertheless one has to face pressing requests for such things as two dozen sausage rolls for the Fur and Feather Whist Drive, or a raffle prize for the Cubs' Social.

It was no surprise then, when Mrs Pringle approached me one morning and asked if I would do her a favour. This polite phrase, accompanied by a slight lessening of malevolence in her expression, was the prelude to my whipping up a sponge for some cause dear to her stony heart, I guessed.

I was right, or nearly so.

'I'm helping Mrs Benson with Cruelty to Children,' she announced. 'Could you give us a bottle of something? It's a good cause, this Cruelty to Children.'

I wondered if a bottle of arsenic, or even castor oil, would be fitting in the circumstances.

'Anything, Mrs Benson says, from whisky to shampoo. Or even home-made wine,' she added.

At that moment the children surged in in a state of wild excitement.

'It's snowing, miss,' they yelled fortissimo.

In the stampede, Ernest stood heavily and painfully upon my foot.

'I'll find you something,' I promised Mrs Pringle, as I retired, wincing.

And if ever anyone needs support for the Prevention of Cruelty to Teachers, I thought, nursing my wounds, I shall be in the forefront.

Fortunately the snow was not severe. One or two flurries during the afternoon soon died out, leaving the playground wet but not white, for which I was thankful. It was good to get home again by the fire on such a cheerless day. I was relishing a cup of tea and Tibby's welcoming purrs, when Mrs Willet arrived.

She is a neat quiet little person and renowned in Fairacre for her domestic efficiency. Mrs Willet's sponge cakes and home-made jam invariably take first prizes at our Flower Show, and if there were awards for laundry work and exquisite mending she would doubtless take those too.

She accepted a cup of tea after some demurring and sat rather primly on the edge of her chair. Tibby rubbed round her lisle-clad legs affectionately, and soon Mrs Willet began to look more relaxed.

'Has Mrs Pringle asked for a bottle?' she said at last.

'Yes. I can find her one quite easily.'

This sounded as though I had a cellar stuffed with strong drink, and as I knew that Mrs Willet and her husband were staunch teetotallers I wondered if she would disapprove.

'Then I hardly like to ask you for anything more, Miss Read, but the truth is I've taken on a book stall at this bazaar of Mrs Benson's, and I wondered if you could spare one.'

'You can have a dozen,' I cried. 'Probably two dozen. I'll bring them down during the week.'

'Bob'll do that,' Mrs Willet assured me. 'You put 'em in a sack, and he'll hump 'em home all right.'

I was not too happy about my books – even rejected ones – ending up in a sack, but said I would have a word with Mr Willet when they were ready.

'And what's happening about the centenary?' asked Mrs Willet. 'Any plans?'

'Not *firm* ones,' I prevaricated. 'Do you remember much about the school when you were here?'

'Quite a bit, though I started school in Caxley. We didn't move out to Fairacre until the end of the Great War, sometime in 1918. I had an auntie that lived in one of those cottages near the post office.'

'What brought you from Caxley?'

'Lack of money,' said Mrs Willet sadly. 'My dad was killed in the January in France, and Mum had three of us at home with her. Mum got a good job helping at the Manor here, so we up-sticks and came to Fairacre.'

'A big change for you.'

'We liked it. Mr Hope was the headmaster here then, and a good kind chap he was although he was on the bottle then, poor soul, and that was the ruin of him. Fairacre was a lot different then – more shops and that. There was a smithy and two bakers, as well as a butcher and the stores. I used to have my dinner at the baker's sometimes.'

'Why was that?'

'Well, once a week my mum and auntie had to stay all day at the Manor. I believe Auntie did a bit of dressmaking there, and Mum had to do the windows. Something extra anyway. Most of the children took sandwiches to school, but there was a lot of horseplay among the big boys and Mr Hope didn't come over to stop 'em, as by rights he should've done. I was fair scared, so Mum made an arrangement that I had two boiled eggs and bread and butter and a cake at Webster's, on the day she was up the Manor.'

'What happened to the other two children?'

'Oh, they were younger, not school age, and went with Mum and Auntie. So they had their dinner in the Manor kitchen. Best meal of the week, Mum said. Always a cut off the joint and vegetables from the kitchen garden, and a great fruit pie to follow, but I wasn't envious. I felt like a queen having my boiled eggs at the shop.'

'With the baker's family?'

'Oh no! Much better than that! There were two or three marble-topped tables for customers. Not that anyone ever came in to eat when I was there, but the Websters did teas for these cyclists that were all about, and ramblers, as they were called before they turned into hikers. Sometimes someone from the village would pop in for a loaf or a pennorth of yeast, and then I'd feel very superior being waited on. My meal cost sixpence, I remember, and I could choose any cake I liked from the window, after the eggs and bread and butter.'

'And what did you choose?'

'Always a doughnut. It was either that, or a currant bun or a queen cake. I reckoned a doughnut was the best value. I had that with a glass of milk. Not bad for sixpence.'

I agreed. Mrs Willet's eyes became dreamy as she looked back almost sixty years.

'There was a lovely picture pinned up on the wall. I think it was an advertisement for Mazawattee tea. There was this lady in a long skirt and a fur stole, with a beautiful hat on top with her Queen Alexandra fluffy fringe just showing.

She was sitting on a park bench, and dangling a little parcel, with "Mazawattee" written on it, from one finger. She had on the most beautiful long suede gloves. I often wondered why she was sitting on a park bench in such gorgeous clothes. It might have dirtied them.'

'Probably collapsed exhausted after carrying a quarter of tea,' I suggested.

'She had a lovely face,' went on Mrs Willet. 'I thought I should like to look like that when I was grown up. But there, it never happened.'

She put down her cup, and began to get up.

'How I do run on! But it's nice to talk of old times. Bob thinks it's a waste of time to hark back, but I enjoy it. That's why I hope you'll be able to think of something for the centenary. We've got a lot to be thankful for in this village, and the school's the real centre of it.'

'It's good to hear you say so,' I told her. 'Never fear! We'll do the thing in style. And I won't forget the books.'

I showed her out into the murky winter dusk, and returned to my fire with much to think about. One day soon, I told myself, I must look through the school log books for some inspiration.

But before I had a chance to do this, Miss Briggs put forward an idea of her own.

'What about dressing the children in the costume of the 1880s, and making the schoolroom much as it was then? We could have copybooks, with pot hooks and hangers, and let them chant their tables, and even have a cane on the teacher's desk.'

I agreed that such a *tableau vivant* would no doubt appeal to the parents, but wondered if it might be rather ambitious.

'Why?' demanded Miss Briggs.

'Rigging out the children, for one thing. Plenty of parents could make the clothes for one, say, but I can't see big families like the Coggses even beginning.'

Miss Briggs began to look mutinous, and I hastily made amends.

'But I do like the idea, and we'll keep it in mind. After all, any brainwaves we have will probably need to be modified. We must remember, though, that space is limited, and if all the children are present there won't be a lot of room for grown-ups.'

My assistant looked slightly less aggressive, and I began to wonder if this would be a good opportunity to discuss her too-prompt departure after school, but decided to postpone the task, as a bevy of infants swarmed in bearing one of their number with a bleeding knee, all bawling as fiercely as the wounded one. It was not the time for a delicate matter of school discipline, but I determined to broach it before the week was out.

Later that day, Miss Briggs approached me, starry-eyed.

'I've had another idea. Perhaps the vicar would dress up as the Reverend Stephen Anderson-Williams. I see from the log book that he was here for the first ten years of the school's existence, and seemed to pop in daily.'

I hardly liked to tell her, after throwing cold water on her earlier idea, that the reverend gentleman she had named was still remembered by the older generation, as the man who had left a perfectly good wife and six young children at his vicarage to run off with a sloe-eyed beauty from Beech Green. He was never seen again, but it was believed that he and his inamorata made a home together in Belgium.

Somehow, I doubted if the present vicar would wish to portray him in our revels. The Reverend Stephen Anderson-Williams would be better forgotten in my opinion, especially as some of his descendants still lived in the Caxley area.

'It's quite a thought,' I said guardedly, and we left it at that.

There was a sudden lull in the bleak weather, and for the best part of a week the sky was a pellucid blue, and the wind from the downs was warm and balmy. The catkins fluttered in the hedge. Bulbs thrust their stubby noses through the soil, and the birds, bright in their courting finery, began looking for nesting places.

We all felt ten years younger, and the children were as happy as sandboys now that they could play outside. Even Mrs Pringle looked a little less dour and sported a new flowered overall.

'Minnie give it to me for Christmas,' she said, when I admired it. 'I was keeping it for best, but what with the sun and this nice bit of spring, I thought why not wear it?'

'Why not indeed,' I agreed.

'Besides,' she added, 'what's the good of hoarding things? I mean, for all we know we may be knocked down by a bus before we have a chance to use our good stuff.'

This sounded more like Mrs Pringle to me. 'Always merry and bright,' as someone sang lugubriously in *The Arcadians*, but at least she had shown herself momentarily in tune with the spring sunshine around her. One must be thankful for small mercies.

I took advantage of this blessing of early warmth and ushered the children out for an afternoon walk. The rooks were wheeling about the high trees, and one or two little birds flew across our path, trailing dry grass and moss in their beaks, intent upon their nest building. There was even a bold bumble bee investigating the ivy on the churchyard wall, and someone said the frogspawn might be starting in the pond. Of course we had to go and see, but there was none there.

I looked at my watch. It said almost three-thirty, and we

set off for school at a brisk pace. There were several things to put away before Mrs Pringle appeared, and grace to be sung before the end of school at a quarter to four.

As we approached the school gate, Miss Briggs's little car appeared. The children scattered to left and right, but I stood my ground. The church clock said three-thirty exactly, and so did my watch.

Miss Briggs peered from the side window.

'Can you spare a minute?' I said. She looked a little annoyed, but duly reversed into the playground.

The children and I entered the school, tidied up, sang: *Now the day is over* and wished each other good afternoon.

Miss Briggs came into the room as the last of the footsteps died away. It was not quite ten to four.

No time like the present, I thought, and invited her to sit down.

'I oughtn't to stop,' she said. 'I'm picking up a friend at four o'clock.'

'This won't take a minute,' I promised her, and began to point out the necessity of staying until all her children were accounted for at the end of the day.

'But the hours are nine till three-thirty,' she protested.

'Not in teaching, they aren't,' I assured her. 'The children are in your care. What would have happened if one had injured himself before I got back? There were seven or eight infants under seven left to their own devices.'

She did not appear particularly contrite, or even fully aware of having been at fault, but I made it clear that she must not leave until my children had collected their younger brothers and sisters, and she went off looking more irritated than chastened.

Well, I had said my piece, I told myself, locking my desk drawers. Now it was up to my assistant to profit from it.

3. March

The 'soft weather', as the Irish say, remained with us, and March came in like the lamb rather than the lion. I was pottering about in the garden after tea, admiring the swelling buds on the lilac bushes, when a car stopped at the gate, and out stepped Miss Quinn.

The little I know of Miriam Quinn I like. She is an extremely hard-working and efficient secretary to an eminant industrialist whose offices are in Caxley. So far, she has managed to stay fairly clear of the multitudinous activities in the village, and one rarely sees her.

She and Joan Benson, her landlady at Holly Lodge, are good friends despite their difference in temperament. Joan, since her husband died recently, has taken on all kinds of public work in Fairacre, and her good humour has endeared her to us all.

This visit from Miriam, I surmised, was something to do with the Caxley Festival. I took her indoors with pleasure and offered her a drink, but she shook her head.

'We've just had a farewell party for one of our staff at the office,' she told me, 'and I've had quite enough for one evening, I think.' She went on to explain her visit which, as I had guessed, was about the festival.

'I hope you aren't going to ask me to open my garden,' I said. 'Not that people might not be delighted to see more weeds than in their own, but I can't compete with real gardeners.'

She laughed, and I thought how attractive she was when her usually serious expression was lit by laughter.

'Don't worry! It's something far less arduous. We're

going to have teas in the village hall, and I'm trying to find out who would be willing to help. Joan's in charge, but would need about a dozen people to make a rota.'

'Oh, I'll willingly help,' I cried, much relieved. 'And if you want a cake, I am rather a dab hand at an almond one.'

'Splendid!' she said, producing a notebook and pencil. I noticed how neat the list was, and how quickly she made her notes. Obviously a treasure in the office at Caxley. No wonder she had been importuned by all the local clubs for help.

'Joan will be so grateful. We've got four names so far, including Mrs Willet who is marvellous, I hear.'

'You couldn't do better,' I assured her.

'What a pretty house this is,' said Miriam.

'I love it,' I said, 'but the snag is, of course, that it's a tied house and I really ought to look for somewhere else for my old age. I keep putting it off, which is quite mad, as house prices get more impossible each week.'

'It's not easy to find a place,' she agreed.

'Would you like to see the rest of it?'

'I'd love to. Houses are a great interest of mine. I was so lucky to find the annexe at Holly Lodge. Nothing in Caxley could compare with it.'

She followed me through the few rooms of the schoolhouse and seemed enchanted with all she saw, pausing at the bedroom windows to exclaim at the superb views which I am lucky enough to enjoy.

'I find this downland country marvellously exhilarating,' she said. 'When I get back from Caxley I feel pretty jaded, but ten minutes in this air, and with these views, and I'm a new woman. The thought of leaving it fills me with despair.'

'But you don't have to leave it, do you?' I asked, puzzled.

She made a grimace.

'I don't know. It will soon be common knowledge, I expect, so that I don't think I'm betraying confidences. Joan is probably moving nearer her daughter whenever anything suitable turns up. She will sell Holly Lodge then, of course. I suppose I could stay on, but I shouldn't care to live at such close quarters with strangers, and in any case Joan would get a much better price without a tenant in the place.'

'She'll be missed,' I said. 'Let's hope she won't have to go for some time. Isn't she happy here?'

'Very happy. But she's about seventy, and getting less and less fond of driving, and I think her daughter feels she should be at hand if her mother were ill. It's all very sensible and understandable, but I dread her going, and dread house-hunting all over again even more.'

'Well, it was nice of you to tell me, and I won't say anything until I hear from other people that it's known in the village. Not that that will take long, knowing Fairacre,' I added.

Miriam laughed and made for the door.

'No secrets in a village!' she agreed, and departed down the path to the car.

One morning, soon after Miriam Quinn's visit, Reg Thorn appeared again with two men from the education office. They wanted to inspect the skylight again, and to see if the roof would stand a more solid structure built upon it.

This sounded hopeful to me. Could Fairacre School really be getting a proper dormer window to replace our temperamental skylight after a hundred years? I readily gave my permission for them to clamber about on the roof, and they departed.

Luckily, the weather was still fine, and apart from a good deal of thumping overhead which produced a light shower

of flaked paint, dead leaves and an assortment of defunct
wasps, spiders and earwigs upon my desk, we managed to
continue our lessons in comparative peace.

The three vanished just before playtime, and I listened to
the children's comments as they imbibed their morning
milk.

'I bet them two men was telling ol' Reg the best way to
do it.'

'What's a dormer anyway?'

'Do it have curtains like a proper window?'

'My auntie up Caxley says dormers lets in the draught
something cruel.'

'D'you reckon we'll get it by the summer?'

'You'll be lucky! What with ol' Reg doin' it?'

It was like hearing their parents talking. Fairacre loves a
new topic. The replacement of our skylight was going to
keep everyone happy for a long time to come.

But not too long, I fervently hoped. I had a feeling that
the fine weather would break the minute the glass was
removed.

Mr Willet was of the same opinion. He was surveying
the school roof when I went across to my house during the
dinner hour.

'That'll never stand nothin' stronger than a skylight, that
roof,' he asserted. 'Stands to reason, all that was gone into
when this place was built. If it wouldn't bear the weight
then, when them beams was new, what chance will it have
now?'

'Perhaps it was too expensive to have a proper window
put in then,' I hazarded.

'What, with all the money the Hurleys put up to help
pay for it? They'd not grudge a few more quid to make the
school ship-shape and Bristol fashion. Always had to be
the best for the Hurleys.'

'Come and look at my broad beans,' I urged, anxious to

change the subject, and to collect a book of Greek myths to read to the children in the afternoon.

He followed me obediently as I led the way.

He studied my two rows of beans with a serious expression.

'You got blackfly comin' on,' he said. 'And them weeds is doing all right too. I better come up for an hour this evening.'

'Thank you,' I said. 'I'd be glad of your help. Have a look round while I nip in to fetch a book.'

He was still plodding morosely round the vegetable patch when I returned. It was unlike him to look so depressed. Could it be the state of my garden? I had been thinking that it looked unusually tidy. Not that it could hold a candle to Mr Willet's own plot, which was always a miracle of neatness and fertility, but not at all bad by my lowly standards.

'See you this evening then,' I said to the pacing figure. 'Any time suits me.'

'Ah!' answered Mr Willet absently, kicking a stone from the grass on to the garden bed. 'I tell you, Miss Read, that skylight was *right* for that roof. The Hurleys would've known, and I'll wager old Reg don't. It's not going to be as simple as they makes out.'

So it was the skylight that was casting this unaccustomed gloom upon Mr Willet! I felt mightily relieved.

'Well, cheer up,' I said, making my way towards the playground. 'That's Reg's look-out, isn't it?'

'It'll be mine before the pesky thing's been up a month or two,' forecast my caretaker. 'I'm the mug as always has to clear up other folk's mess!'

As he was still eyeing my weeds, I forebore to comment, but carried my Greek myths across to school in prudent silence.

*

News of Joan Benson's departure from Holly Lodge was very soon common gossip in the village, as Miriam had forecast.

The first to tell me was the vicar. 'A grievous loss!' he said. 'We were all so delighted when she and her husband and mother arrived, but now we must lose the last of the three. I wonder when she is moving?'

I was unable to tell him, but Mrs Pringle told me an hour or two later.

'Getting down to her daughter's as soon as she can,' she informed me. 'Going to look out for a little place down there. A bungalow, I don't doubt. Stairs get somethin' cruel as you get on, and she's got a touch of arthritis already.'

I said, somewhat shortly, that it was the first I had heard of it.

Mrs Pringle continued undismayed: 'Holly Lodge ought to fetch a good price on the market. Nice garden and that, and you can call your soul your own with that holly hedge all round. Don't get no busybodies peering in like I do at home.'

This was a side swipe at her immediate neighbour, and I was careful to make no comment. It would soon have got back in Fairacre, and I do my best to steer a steady course.

'I wonder what Miss Quinn will do?' was her next surmise. 'She won't find it easy to find as quiet a place as that little flat of hers, and I don't suppose she earns enough to buy anything outright, do you?'

'I have no knowledge of Miss Quinn's income nor of her future plans,' I said stiffly. Was there no way of stopping this gossip? Evidently not, for the lady continued.

'That little hovel near Miss Waters is in *The Caxley Chronicle* this week for thirty thousand pounds. I ask you! Who'd buy that shack anyway? I can remember when old

Perce Tilling bought it for three hundred pounds, and then we told him a fool and his money was soon parted. Not that Perce cared. He'd just won a packet at Caxley races, and his old auntie who kept the shop at Beech Green had just died, and they found over four hundred under the mattress when they lifted her into her coffin, so Perce got that as well. Not fair really, as that daughter of hers, although no better than she should be when it came to American soldiers, did do her best by her mum, and kept her lovely and clean, right to the end.'

'You got a minute?' shouted Mr Willet from the door. Once again he was my saviour, and I escaped thankfully from Mrs Pringle's reminiscences.

Within the week I had been told by Mr Lamb at the post office that it was a great shame Mrs Benson had got to give up. The place was too big for her, no doubt, now her husband and mother were dead. Still, it should fetch a tidy sum these days. He reckoned anything between thirty and forty thousand.

The butcher, cleaving lamb chops, told me between hacks that it was a pity Mrs Benson's daughter was in trouble of some sort, and such a nice old lady had got to sell up and go to help. On the other hand, this was the right time to sell, and she would probably clear forty or fifty thousand.

Mr Roberts, the farmer, said that we should miss Joan Benson. She'd been a nice body to have in the village, and he was sorry to hear her health was obliging her to leave Holly Lodge. Nevertheless, that was a tidy little property and on a nice bit of rich soil, as his father had always said, a fair treat for root crops. To his mind it should fetch somewhere round fifty thousand.

The price of property in our village has always occasioned the greatest interest. It was obvious that the amount finally given for Holly Lodge would provide Fairacre with an enthralling topic in the future.

It so happened that I met Joan Benson returning from the grocer's shop about this time. She was hurrying along, as round and cheerful as a robin, and put down her basket to talk to me.

'I've just been told,' she said, looking amused, 'that my house should fetch between fifty and sixty thousand pounds. As it isn't even on the market yet, I'm rather tickled. Does Fairacre always rush ahead like this with conjectures?'

'Always,' I told her. 'It's all part of the fun!'

Amy rang up one evening to invite me to dinner to meet the poets who were to take part in the Caxley Festival in May.

'I thought it would be a good idea for them to see where it would be held, and perhaps to meet each other.'

'How many are there?'

'Well, I'm sorry to say I can only rustle up a couple. There were going to be four, but one is having a nervous breakdown, poor thing, and the other is touring the United States with his poetry programme. What stamina!'

'Americans are noted for their strength and energy,' I told her.

'Not the *Americans*! The poet, I meant. He looks such a weed too, as though walking up the steps of Caxley Town Hall would finish him off, but there he is – all eight stone of him – bouncing about all over America. I can't get over it. Not that Tim Ferdinand, who will be coming, is much sturdier.'

'How's your weight going?' I asked, reminded of Amy's slimming efforts by these poets' obvious fragility.

'Don't speak of it. I seem to have put on three pounds in the last week.'

'The scales have gone wrong.'

'Do you really think so?' Amy sounded wonderfully cheered. 'I hadn't thought of that. I'll try yours when I come over.'

'Please do, but I warn you that mine are almost half a stone too much, and friends come tottering downstairs looking demented until I explain it to them.'

'I'll remember. By the way, as the poets are so thin on the ground I've found a nice pianist as makeweight, and I'm just wondering if I could ask that marvellous singer Jean Cole who sang at the Fairacre festival some years ago.'

'It's flying rather high,' I said doubtfully. 'I think she only came because she was a relation of Major Gunning's, and he left some time ago.'

'Do you know where he went?'

'I could find out. I've an idea he's in a nursing home or private hotel somewhere not too far away. The vicar might know.'

'Be a lamb and see what you can do. Two poets, a pianist and Jean Cole should fill the bill beautifully.'

I promised to do my best.

'See you on Thursday week then. Long skirt to do honour to my four-course dinner, and make yourself as smart as possible.'

I blew a raspberry down the line to my bossy old friend.

I spent the rest of the evening looking out bottles and books for Joan Benson's bazaar. The bottles presented no problem. I had three bottles of tomato ketchup, a comestible of which I partake sparingly, so two of those went into the basket, and a bottle of home-made lemon essence.

The upstairs cupboard yielded a bottle of shampoo, and another of pungent scent, called *Dusky Allure* which had been given me by one of the children. As the said child had now moved from the district, I felt I could safely donate it. One has to be careful in a village; reputations have been ruined over just such little matters. Not a bad haul, I thought, surveying my five bottles. I only hoped I did not win any of them back again.

But the books occupied me for the rest of the evening. I began in a fine crusading spirit, ruthlessly putting aside half a dozen novels which I told myself I should never read again. It seemed prudent, though, to cast a cursory glance over them, and in no time I was deep in one which I had completely forgotten and found enthralling. I put it back on the shelf to finish later.

Meanwhile, crouched as I was on the floor, I became horribly stiff, and decided to look through the rest in my armchair. At a quarter to ten I realized that I had galloped through most of them, and five were put aside as absolutely essential to my needs. One book alone remained at hand for Mrs Willet's stall. I decided that I had done enough sorting for one evening. Tomorrow I would be firm and start again. It would be a good thing to clear out the bookshelves, but now bed called.

I took a final look at the rows of books. Would anyone read that life of Marlborough? Or that terrible edition of *Lorna Doone* with illustrations presumably executed in weak cocoa? And what about *Whitaker's Almanack* for 1953, and that glossy American cookery book full of recipes about squash and scallions and clams, and every one of them in cupfuls? Any takers, I wondered?

Who would have thought that giving away books would prove so tiring? It would have to wait until tomorrow.

I went to bed carrying my first rejected book with me.

The next morning I determined to find out when Fairacre School had first opened its doors to the children of the village. The forthcoming celebration, once we had decided on its nature, should take place approximately around the same time of year, I felt.

The earliest log book is a battered affair, leather covered and with beautifully mottled endpapers. It weighs several pounds, and the ink has now faded to fawn. The entries make fascinating reading.

I was mightily relieved to discover that the school opened at the beginning of December in 1880. If we were to celebrate the occasion then at least we knew that it must be an indoor affair. No playground nonsense, wondering if the heavens would open in a summer shower. The longer I live in a village, the more I marvel at the touching faith with which folk organize outside affairs in our climate. June can be cruelly chilly, and I well remember that on Coronation Day on 2 June the most joyful moment was when we lit the bonfire and could huddle round the welcome blaze.

No one would expect anything outdoors at the beginning of December, so that cleared the ground nicely in my opinion. Something in the school must be arranged and, if need be, repeated to accommodate all the parents and friends.

The first headmistress was a Miss Richards, and her sister looked after the infants. Judging by the first entry, the opening of the school had been awaited for some time. The builders had not finished their work in the time allotted. Could some of Reg Thorn's forebears have been employed, I wondered?

The two ladies obviously had difficulty with discipline. There are a good many entries describing canings, and one John Pratt who seems to have been a sore trial and quite unmoved by frequent chastisement. What became of him, I wondered? He was evidently a resourceful boy, for he was discovered 'putting on the Hands of the Clock with the greatest Audacity' in July 1882, and a little later released a frog during the vicar's lesson on the Good Samaritan.

The two sisters resigned in 1885, giving their reason as ill health, but the boisterous spirits of their country pupils must have had something to do with it.

A widow and her daughter came next, and this pattern of a headmistress and woman assistant continued for some years. It was interesting to note that for all its hundred years Fairacre School had remained a two-teacher establishment. There must have been some odd pairings, I guessed, but probably no more difficult than my present companion-in-harness, Miss Briggs. Two women, thus yoken, must learn to pull together to their mutual advantage and that of the school.

I closed the log book and replaced it in the desk drawer with a feeling of relief. There would be plenty of time to work out something to celebrate our centenary, and at least it would not clash with the Caxley Festival in May, which was showing signs of impinging on our rural tranquillity.

I was slamming back the drawer when the vicar entered. He came to the point at once, after greeting the children and admiring the progress of our hyacinth grown over water.

'As a child I used to grow acorns over medicine bottles,' he told me. 'I had a splendid collection one year.' His eyes grew misty at the recollection, but he returned to the reason for his visit. 'Have you any idea when the school first opened? I confess I can find no reference to it anywhere.'

I told him, with some pride, and his face cleared.

'Ah! That is good news! It gives me plenty of time to arrange a suitable service. Do you think the first Sunday in December, in the afternoon, would be a good idea, or perhaps an evening one during the week?'

I wondered privately whether his parishioners would

prefer to forego their Sunday-afternoon nap, or to turn out on a dark December evening, leaving their cosy firesides for the chill of St Patrick's church. It was difficult to offer advice, and I said so.

Luckily the vicar appeared to make up his own mind. 'On the whole, I think an afternoon service would be best. We want the children to attend, after all, and it would be a great pity if they were deprived just because it was their bedtime.'

I did not like to point out to our innocent pastor that the majority of the children would be glued to their television sets until about ten o'clock or later, imbibing all sorts of dubious knowledge, no doubt.

'There's a lot to be said for a service during the hours of daylight,' I replied diplomatically.

And we left it at that.

'By the way,' I said, as I accompanied him to the door. 'Do you happen to know Major Gunning's address?'

I told him about Amy's hope of inviting Jean Cole to dinner. He looked doubtful.

'She's so much in demand,' he said.

'I know.'

'But I can give you the major's address. He's at a private hotel in Caxley. It's either Ash Tree Hotel, or Elm Court or possibly Hawthorn House. Something arboreal, I know. I will look it up and let you have it, Miss Read.'

He gave a sigh.

'This Caxley Festival is, no doubt, an excellent project, but it does seem to make an inordinate amount of *planning*.'

I agreed, and returning to my class, thought that centenary celebrations shared the same problems.

4. April

Amy's party took place on the second day of the month.

After a boisterous morning which toppled the crocuses and blew the rooks off course, the sun came out, and by the time I set off all was tranquil. The western sky was dappled with little pink clouds as the sun went down, and the air was so clear and still that I could see a range of hills some twenty miles away to the south.

Obedient to Amy's request, I had donned a long black skirt bought at Caxley's most favoured outfitters, and identical to quite half a dozen I had observed on various local friends during the past winter. The blouse that topped it was of black and white silk which I thought looked rather fetching, but as it had a back zip I was resigned to undertaking violent contortions to do it up every time I wore it, and was beginning to wonder how long it would be before such exercises were beyond me.

As usual, I was the first to arrive. Amy greeted me with unusual affection.

'You look splendid! Truly elegant! Come and see the table. I'm rather proud of the flowers.'

She led the way into the dining room, and it certainly was a vision of delight. Daffodils and narcissi scented the room, and in the centre of the table was a magnificent arrangement of freesias and miniature daffodils in shades of cream and gold.

Amy stood surveying it, a look of supreme satisfaction on her face.

'It's perfect,' I told her.

'And that damask tablecloth was my grandmother's. It's

a devil to launder, and so it doesn't get used very often, but those Victorians had some good ideas about dressing a table.'

'Do you remember Mrs Beeton's illustration for a simple supper party? Three epergnes of red roses down the centre, and smilax trailing everywhere?'

'Our old edition had a picture of a tray for an invalid,' recalled Amy. 'There were two silver trumpet-shaped flower vases with carnations, as well as two or three dishes complete with silver covers, a coffee pot, milk jug and sugar bowl. I don't think you could lift the thing, let alone stagger upstairs with it. But I must say it looked superb.'

'I pity anyone being taken ill in my house. A plate of toast and a mug of tea would be about my limit.'

'James has occasionally brought me my breakfast in bed when I've been too ill with flu, or something equally horrid, to get up. He can manage very thick bread and butter, with the crusts rather touchingly cut off, and the marmalade pot, and a cup of tea with most of it in the saucer by the time he's negotiated the stairs. But I certainly don't get carnations, and to be honest, I don't think I should appreciate them in the state I'm in when I have to stay in bed.'

'Now tell me who's coming,' I said when we returned to the sitting room.

'The two poets I told you about, and Betty Mason the pianist. Jean Cole is on tour in Belgium. I managed to get in touch with Major Gunning, thanks to you, and he says she'll be back next week and he'll find out her plans.'

'He won't forget,' I assured her. 'He was the mainstay of dozens of our village committees.'

'I invited him tonight, but he says he's become rather too old for parties. A shame really, he sounds a dear.'

'And James?'

'No James, I'm afraid. At a company dinner in South

Shields. But I've invited Horace Umbleditch to make up the six. He's giving an organ recital in the church as part of the Caxley Festival, so he'll enjoy meeting some of the others, I hope. And anyway, he's devoted to you.'

'He's nothing of the sort!' I protested. 'I hardly know the fellow!'

'Well, I know better. And he's moved into such a charming house in the school grounds now, and could well do with a wife.'

'Amy, you are incorrigible! You know I have no wish to marry, nor presumably has Horace Umbleditch, and if he had, I'm sure he could find someone younger and keener than I am. Do leave us happy old spinsters and bachelors in peace!'

'Hoity-toity!' cried Amy, as the front-door bell rang. I watched her as she hurried to answer it, admiring the back view of her elegant cream silk caftan. Had she chosen it for tonight's occasion as the perfect complement to her flower arrangements? Knowing Amy, I guessed that she had.

She returned with Betty Mason in tow, a short rather dumpy person wearing black with a sparkling necklace. She had beautifully waved silver hair and a soft, powdery pink and white complexion which reminded me of marshmallows. During the evening I was to discover that she was as sweet and gentle as her looks.

We had scarcely greeted each other when Amy was called to the door again, and Horace Umbleditch arrived. There was no need for introductions as Betty and Horace knew each other, and were soon deep in discussion about the best choice of music for a country festival.

Then, turning to me, Horace asked if I had heard the good news about his sister Irene.

'Henry Mawne told me,' I said, and then wondered if the good news he spoke of was about the proposed marriage to David Mawne after all. Perhaps it was something quite different – a new post, maybe, or a fantastic win on the pools, always supposing that Irene went in for such things.

However, I did not have to endure suspense for long, as Horace said that the wedding was to be in early June, at a registry office, and no doubt I should see them before then as they proposed to stay for a few days with Henry during the Caxley Festival.

'It is marvellous news,' I agreed, glad to be right for once. 'And where will they live?'

'For the moment in David's flat, but I expect they will move further out sometime. It's not much fun there for Simon in the holidays, and I'm sure Irene will look forward to making a home elsewhere.'

Away from the haunting horrors which that flat must hold for David, I thought privately, and for young Simon who had seen his mother at her most terrifying in those surroundings.

Amy came in and glanced at the clock, which said a quarter to eight. 'I do hope the others haven't lost their way. They are coming together.'

'Tim Ferdinand's usually pretty punctual,' said Horace.

'Oh, you know him! I hadn't realized that.'

'Very slightly. He came to the school one evening to read poetry to the boys. They were remarkably well-behaved.'

No one knew quite how to react to the last remark, and Amy said she must go and check that the crab was all right, conjuring up visions of a sickly crustacean with a bottle of medicine alongside.

'Something smells delicious,' commented Betty kindly.

'I just hope it won't be overdone,' said Amy, setting off for the kitchen. 'It's in a light cheese sauce, and you know how easily that can dry up.'

'Amy is the best cook I know,' said Horace with enthusiasm. 'After school meals, all cabbage and custard, the food here is sheer ambrosia.'

'It's so nice,' said Betty, 'to find people interested in food. I can't bear those who profess to have a mind above it, particularly when you have spent all day and a great deal of money in preparing something you think they will enjoy.'

The bell rang again, and we heard voices in the hall.

'I can't *think*,' we heard a despairing voice say, 'where I went wrong, but we took a short cut and ended up on the downs. It really is too bad the way some of these roads simply peter out into sheep tracks. A hundred apologies, Amy dear.'

'All is forgiven,' said Amy, 'and you really aren't late at all. Come and meet the others.'

She ushered in a short tubby man with a florid complexion set off by a neat white moustache. He could have been taken for a retired colonel or a particularly kindly bank manager. Perhaps he was, I thought, and simply wrote poems in his spare time on the back of Queen's Regulations or the bank's blotting-paper.

'John Chandler,' said Amy. 'He has just published his third book of poems.'

We all gave cries of admiration and welcomed our fellow guest.

'And Timothy Ferdinand. You know Horace, I believe, and this is Betty Mason the pianist, and Miss Read.'

We made more polite noises and I thought how much more like a poet he looked. For one thing, he was painfully thin and pale, as Amy had told me, with a wobbly Adam's apple which showed to advantage as he wore an open-necked shirt above blue jeans carefully fringed at the ankle. I was glad to see he had socks on under the inevitable sandals, and his hands were clean.

He looked a pleasant, if vague, young man, and still seemed to be brooding about the way he became lost on his journey.

'It happens to us all,' I assured him. 'It's those crossroads at Springbourne. Someone said once that it seems to be moved overnight. As a matter of fact, some young people did turn the signpost round one night, and confusion was worse confounded.'

He looked a little happier.

'You're quite right. It was at the crossroads we went wrong. But why not say "No thoroughfare", or "Downs only"?'

'I suppose the reasoning *is* that there is a road for about a mile before it dwindles into a track.'

'Possibly,' said Timothy doubtfully. He took out a rather grubby red and white spotted handkerchief and polished his sherry glass in a preoccupied way. I was glad that Amy was out of the room at the time.

Before long she returned, and we talked about the Caxley Festival while the most delicious smells wreathed around us.

The attitude of the two poets towards this event varied considerably, although both agreed, somewhat vehemently, that Caxley needed 'to be awakened'. John Chandler looked upon it as a useful way of becoming known to a larger number of readers than before.

'Good publicity,' he said briskly. 'Might even sell a dozen or so extra books. Though one can't help feeling that at these affairs one is preaching to the converted. Still, it all helps.'

Timothy Ferdinand's attitude was less commercial.

'Oh surely,' he cried, 'it is the artist and his work that really matters! He needs an audience to stimulate him, and I think that the festival will do that very well.'

'Let's carry on this discussion while we eat,' said Amy.

We followed our hostess into the pretty dining room and confronted our sizzling ramekins.

'If you don't like crab,' said Amy, 'there is melon ready on the sideboard.'

Only Betty asked if she might change. 'I adore crab, but can't digest it,' she said apologetically, and John rose swiftly to make the replacement.

I thought how sensible Amy was to offer an alternative to one's first course. So often the hostess has gone to no end of trouble to produce something rather exotic, often with shell fish or avocado pear which many people cannot take. I myself have several times been faced with taramasalata which, with the best will in the world, I cannot get down. If only I had been offered a slice of melon or a nice little tot of orange or tomato juice waiting on the sideboard, how much happier I should have been!

Horace Umbleditch sat beside me and John Chandler opposite. They were both exuberant talkers and Amy and I had little to do in the way of keeping the conversation going. Timothy Ferdinand still seemed slightly distraught, at the foot of the table, facing Amy, but gulped down his crab as though he had not seen food for weeks, and nodded abstractedly at Betty's gentle remarks.

Cold turkey and ham with a handsome salad followed the crab, and a dish of mammoth baked potatoes with butter melting in their floury tops. As Amy served us, I was amused to notice that Timothy was engrossed in cleaning between the prongs of his perfectly spotless fork by inserting them busily in the edge of Amy's beautiful damask tablecloth. He seemed quite unaware of anything amiss. His periodic nods at Betty's gallant monologue continued as before, as with eyes on his work he polished assiduously.

Whether Amy saw him or not, I could not say, but she continued serving with her usual charm, whilst commenting on the possibility of getting Jean Cole to attend the poetry reading during the festival week.

Fortunately, the arrival of his main course saw the cessation of Timothy's cleansing operations, and he fell to with a will and did not seem to feel the need to polish anything else during the sweet and cheese courses.

At last he leant back and gave a sigh of contentment. 'What a perfect dinner! I hardly ever sit down to a meal when I'm alone, and certainly never to one as splendid as this.'

'But don't you get hungry?' enquired Amy.

'I suppose I do,' replied Timothy, looking about him vaguely. 'I eat an apple or a biscuit sometimes. Anything that's lying about, you know.'

No wonder he looked so emaciated, I thought.

Conversation then became concentrated upon the form of Amy's proposed evening, and later she took us all into the drawing room to see the best way of arranging things for the great night.

John Chandler appeared outstandingly practical about this, pointing out the best place for the piano with relation to the lighting and the french windows which, with any luck, might be open to admit the warm evening air, scented with roses and stocks. He also suggested seating arrangements which would ensure the greatest number of people being at ease, and reminded me yet again of a military commander deploying his resources to the best advantage.

Timothy did not contribute much to the plans, but sipped his coffee thoughtfully, only surfacing once to remark that it was a blessing no microphone would be needed in a room this size as he had a horror of the things, and had been hurt by falling over one once, and hurt even more by the B.B.C. mechanic's remarks about the accident.

This led to a general discussion about whether it was a

good thing to understand machinery, or whether it was better to disclaim all knowledge at the outset of how to deal with the objects, and to let someone else tackle the problem.

Eventually the delicate task of allotting time for each artist's performance was undertaken, and it was agreed that roughly half an hour, give or take five minutes, for each, should ensure a full evening's pleasure, and that it was up to each performer to rehearse his own contribution to fix the time it would take.

By eleven o'clock the company had dispersed, looking happy and well fed.

Amy turned down my offer to help with the washing up. Evidently, unheard by me and probably by everyone else in Amy's beautifully soundproof house, her daily help had been hard at it and the kitchen awaited the morrow as spotless as ever.

'Do you think it went well?' asked Amy, on the door-step.

'Everything – but *everything*,' I assured her, as I let in the clutch, 'was absolutely perfect.'

I was delighted to have a letter from the office, a day or two later, to inform me that work on the new window to replace the present skylight would begin at the end of term and should be completed before the beginning of the summer term.

This was good news indeed, although I should have preferred to read '*will* be completed' rather than that cautious '*should* be completed'. However, it was better perhaps to face the probability of a half-finished job than to be disappointed later.

Mrs Pringle shared Mr Willet's doubts about Reg Thorn's ability to do the job at all, let alone to a deadline even as vague as this one.

'What he done to my poor sister-in-law in Caxley you'd never believe,' she assured me. 'You'd think he'd feel downright sorry for a widow woman as suffers something so cruel with arthritis in her hands that she hasn't done her back hair for years now. She told me herself as Reg promised faithful to have her straightened up by last Easter. He'd only got the porch to put to rights. Bob Willet would have done it in two days flat, but Reg hung it out, just when the wind was in the east, fairly scouring out Peg's hall with the front door off, and the bill – which came pretty smartish, I can tell you – was twice the estimate, and give poor old Peg indigestion for a week.'

'Let's hope he's improved since then,' I replied.

Mr Willet, who had joined us, snorted with disgust.

'We'll be lucky to get that dratted dormer by next winter, and then I don't reckon it'll work. If there ain't trouble with the roof I'll eat my hat.'

I refused to be depressed by my two Job's comforters. Nothing could be worse, I felt, than the present ancient skylight. I acknowledged the office's letter in enthusiastic terms, and looked forward to seeing the workmen on the job before the Easter holidays.

I felt less enthusiastic about Miss Briggs's progress in the infants' room. To be sure, she did not rush away at three-thirty as she had done previously, but I rarely saw her smile, she shouted at the babies who, naturally, became noisier than ever, and she made no response to any of my overtures. Mr Willet's early summing up of the young lady as 'a fair old lump of a girl' was true.

It was difficult to know how to improve matters. Over the years, I had worked with dozens of infants' teachers with just the screen between us. Some had been shy, some bold, some flighty, but all had been fairly cheerful, and some outstandingly gifted. A two-teacher school must be

harmonious. There is no getting away from each other, which is possible in a large establishment, and I was at a loss to know how to overcome the girl's sulkiness.

Was she ill perhaps, I wondered? Was she in love? Was she homesick? Or had she realized that she was in a job she disliked, and worried about how to get out of it?

As far as I could find out, she had few friends in Caxley and had not joined any clubs or societies. She must be lonely, I felt, and her digs, though adequate, were not particularly comfortable, I gathered.

I should have to have a word with her sometime, I supposed gloomily. Only a week or two of the present term remained, and she was having a holiday in France at Easter. With any luck she would return with more zest to Fairacre School.

I did not need much persuading to put off this problem until her return, telling myself – not for the first time – that things might sort themselves out. My faith in the power of destiny to resolve my problems is touching, but usually misplaced.

The April weather, which had been kindly, now switched to the other extreme and became violently windy, with sudden vicious storms which scoured the countryside, dowsing newborn lambs and tossing the daffodils to the ground.

The skylight dripped steadily during these onslaughts, and the worst of the storms always seemed to coincide with playtime, so that the children were obliged to spend their break indoors, much to everyone's annoyance.

Several new puddles appeared in the playground, and on the rare occasions when the children spent a few minutes outside a new game had been devised, called, I gathered, 'Splashem'. This involved jumping in the deepest part of a puddle just as someone passed, preferably an infant too small to retaliate and likely to get more of him drenched, and then to enjoy not only the victim's discomfiture, but also the hilarious glee of the onlookers.

It was a game I did my best to stamp out promptly, but not before several cross mothers had called to complain about sopping clothes and squelchy shoes.

On one of the stormiest days, the dinner lady slipped over in the playground, all the gravy was spilled, her knee was badly grazed and her tights ruined. Miss Briggs took care of the school while I rendered first-aid in the schoolhouse. She seemed more agitated about the loss of the gravy than her own injuries.

'I could easily pour some of Beech Green's into a jug for you,' she offered, as I dabbed at her knee with TCP.

'Don't worry, it won't hurt us to go short for once. This skirt is soaked. Would you like to borrow one?'

The offer was accepted, and she went off dry if not particularly elegant, and full of apologies.

Mr Annett, the headmaster at Beech Green, and also choirmaster and organist at Fairacre, called on choir night to tell me that Miss Clare was staying with them.

'She's not too bad,' he began, shaking a wet umbrella energetically, 'but Isobel found her with a heavy cold yesterday when she called, and persuaded her to have a day or two in our spare bed.'

'You are good Samaritans,' I said.

'Not a bit. But come and see her if you can.'

'I'll come tomorrow if it suits you.'

'Fine. We'll look forward to it.'

He sprinted churchwards, and I went indoors out of the beastly wind. This was no weather for poor frail Dolly Clare, I felt, but was comforted to think of her in such safe hands at Beech Green.

If anything, the weather was wilder still when I drove the few miles from Fairacre to Beech Green. The windscreen wipers could scarcely keep pace with the torrent of rain which lashed the car. Young leaves and scraps of early blossom littered the leafy road as though it were an autumn evening. A fast running rivulet ran each side of the lane, and every puddle sent up a shower of drops, reminding me of 'Splashem' and my naughty boys.

The few people I passed on the road were well wrapped up in waterproof garments ranging from sou'westers to wellingtons. I only saw one umbrella, and that was causing its owner considerable trouble. In rough weather, our downland winds can soon rip such a thing to pieces, and it is wiser to have one's hands free to tighten a headscarf or to turn up a raincoat collar against the onslaught.

I found Miss Clare sitting by a cheerful fire. She was dressed, and had a pretty lacy shawl round her shoulders.

'Isobel had to go out,' she told me. 'She is giving a talk over at Springbourne and I wouldn't let her put it off. Really, I'm quite rested now after two nights and one whole day in bed.'

She certainly looked very well, though as thin as ever, but her eyes were bright and I think she was enjoying the company of the Annetts.

'They are so kind,' she went on. 'And the more I know of them the more I am reminded of my early teaching days when Mr and Mrs Hope looked after me so well.'

'Was that the headmaster who had to leave Fairacre?'

Miss Clare nodded sadly. 'He was a gentle soul, and very musical like the Annetts, but they lost their only child when she was twelve or so, and he never got over it. He took to the bottle, you know, and left soon after the Great War in 1919, if I remember rightly.'

'You remember the war well enough,' I said.

'Too well,' she said. 'Not only because I lost my dear Arnold in France, but because of the appalling number of young men from here who never came back. One of the saddest sights in Fairacre School was the black armbands worn by so many of the children. And the tears! You would see some little mite busy writing, and then the pen would stop, and the head would go down and the crying begin. It was dreadful to feel so helpless in the face of such sorrow. Mr Hope felt it all terribly. Sometimes I wonder if that was another reason for his taking to drink.'

'He didn't drink in school?'

'No, thank goodness! He made up for it at home, and was simply morose and befuddled in school towards the end. He still worked hard though, and did a great deal to help the war effort, and saw that the children helped too. Why, I remember that even the youngest babies were set to fraying pieces of white cotton and linen with a darning needle to make field dressings. And of course we all put as much as we could spare – which wasn't much, in those days – into War Savings stamps.'

'But at least you were spared bombings and rushing into air-raid shelters in that war.'

'We saw practically nothing of the war in Fairacre,' agreed Miss Clare, 'and I think, despite the horror stories in the newspapers, that there was less real hatred towards the Germans. We prayed every morning for the war to end, and I daresay we realized that German children were doing the same. We *disliked* them, of course, and *intensely* and I remember Mr Hope taking a grammar lesson at the other end of the classroom. He was trying to get the children to stop using the word "got" – with small success, as you might imagine. He wrote it on the blackboard, and crossed it through. "Got, got, got," he cried. "A horrible word! It must be German! Simply leave it out, and say: 'I *have* a pen! I *have* a new nib!' Understand?" And one of the Bryant boys, a real little gipsy said: "I ain't got neither, sir!" and everyone broke into laughter, including Mr Hope.'

'He sounds a good chap,' I said. 'A pity he had to leave.'

'A tragedy,' agreed Dolly. 'He was as much a casualty of war as my dear Arnold.'

She fingered the gold locket which hung under the lacy shawl. She wore it constantly, and I knew that it contained a photograph of the red-haired young man who had shared the fate of thousands of others whose names were written upon country memorials, and in the hearts of those who loved them.

*

'Heard the latest?' enquired Mr Willet the next morning. 'About the vicar?'

Elevated to rural dean? Broken a leg? Off on holiday? All these dramatic possibilities leapt to mind before Mr Willet spoke again.

'He's going to keep *bees*. I only hope he knows what he's letting himself in for. My old gran had three of those straw skep hives on an old table by her bottom hedge, and by gum, you didn't dare go near 'em to scythe the grass or pick a few runner beans nearby. Fair vicious they was.'

'I expect he's gone into all that.'

'I doubt it. Mr Mawne's been eggin' him on, and got him a couple of hives from some chap over at Bent who's giving up. Seen the light, I reckon. Why, I remember getting some of my gran's bees up my jersey as a kid, and havin' swellings like pudden basins.'

'They tell me that's good for rheumatism.'

Mr Willet snorted.

'Them old wives' tales! My gran had rheumatics something terrible and I bet she was stung often enough. She still told them old bees all that went on, like you hear about. She told 'em about Grandad dying in Caxley Hospital of the dropsy, and about the grandchildren being born. Funny really. People says bees are wise, but the more I hear about 'em the more I wonder. Did you know they goes for people dressed in blue?'

'Never heard of it.'

'No, nor I bet you haven't heard as they don't like compost heaps or bonfires or mowing the grass and a lot of other things you finds in a garden. Pesky little objects! I don't envy the vicar, that I don't!'

'But think of all the lovely honey,' I said.

'Bet you a dollar they'll be getting rape honey. Mr Roberts usually has a good field of that – you know, that blazin' yellow stuff.'

I said I knew what rape looked like. I had not lived in the country all these years without –

Mr Willet interrupted me.

'All right, all right! All I'm saying is that the vicar will have to take his honey off smartish if it's rape, or it'll gum up the whole works. Terrible stuff to extract, as my old gran could tell him, if she'd been spared. No, he don't know what he's letting himself in for, and I only hope he's got a blue bag for banging on the stings.'

'Can you still get a blue bag?'

'I doubt it,' said Mr Willet. He sighed and moved off. After a few steps he stopped and called across the play-ground:

'Hope you aren't thinkin' of startin' bees,' he shouted. 'That's one thing I'm not helping you with, I can tell you.'

During the last day or two of term, I turned over in my mind the snippets of history that I had heard from Dolly Clare. Somewhere here there was the theme for our cen-tenary celebrations, I felt sure.

To give Miss Briggs her due, the idea of dressing the children in the costume of 1880 had some merit. Perhaps we could have just two children in costume telling Fairacre School's story in each decade? Or, more practically, a boy and girl of each of the five reigns – six, if you included Edward VIII – through which the school had passed, suitably apparelled for their particular narrations.

It would be best if we could let the whole school take part, and perhaps a song or poem typical of each period could intersperse the narration. I discussed my nebulous ideas with Miss Briggs, who seemed remarkably co-operative for once. Perhaps her impending holiday in France was having a stimulating effect.

'Have you fixed a date?' she enquired sensibly.

'Sometime in the first week in December,' I told her.

'And for two performances definitely, otherwise we shan't have room for everyone. I thought parents of infants one afternoon, and the others the next.'

'What a good idea! And perhaps we could combine it with the tea party the children usually give at Christmas.'

'That's a thought,' I agreed.

The Christmas party for parents, with the children acting as hosts, is a long-standing tradition in the school. Sometimes we are hopelessly overcrowded; dividing the party into a two-day event might help considerably. I looked at my assistant with new respect. At times she was quite bright, I thought.

'Of course, there's heaps of time for making arrangements,' she said.

'We'll have to start pretty early,' I assured her. 'We must know what we propose to do next term so that the mothers can think about costumes, and it looks to me as though the whole of the autumn term will be devoted to rehearsing, whatever we decide upon.'

'Let's hope the dormer window will be done by then,' said Miss Briggs, watching a steady drip dropping into a bucket by my desk.

'It had better be!' I said grimly.

Mercifully, the rough weather subsided as suddenly as it had arrived, and the last day of term ended in a clear, serene evening.

Its blissful tranquillity matched my own feelings. The empty school basked in the golden rays of the setting sun. The rooks' cawing was the only sound above the tidy playground, and Tibby and I sauntered in the garden relishing our solitude. The narcissi wafted heady draughts of fragrance towards us. The grape hyacinths were a sea of blue in the shrubbery, and some fine scarlet tulips, straight as guardsmen, towered above them. What if the groundsel and dandelions and chickweed were making steady progress? With the holidays ahead I could soon root them out.

The hooting of a car horn brought me back to earth, and I found Amy at the door.

'I've been shopping in Oxford,' she said, 'and thought I'd call on my way home. Is it convenient, or are you having a cocktail party or anything?'

'Don't be funny,' I begged her. 'Whenever have you caught me preparing for a cocktail party?'

'You never know,' replied Amy vaguely. 'How pretty your garden looks.'

We strolled happily around my small plot, enjoying the unusual calm and warmth.

'Do you want to see my new purchases?' enquired Amy, as we made our way back to the house.

She dived into the car and emerged with two exotic-looking dress boxes which she carried into the house. There seemed to be half a hundredweight of tissue paper in each one, but at last the garments were revealed. One was a set of glossy underwear, petticoat, knickers and brassiere in what was called, in my youth, oyster satin. The other was a stunning three-piece in silk jersey, cream in colour with delicate gold decorations at hem and neck.

'Well!' I exclaimed. 'They are all truly gorgeous!'

'So they should be at the ghastly price I had to pay for them. Now I'm beginning to wonder if they are a trifle young for me.'

'Rubbish!' I told her. 'You're a very good-looking woman, as well you know, and can wear anything. You always could.'

'So could you, my dear,' said Amy kindly. 'You were really quite pretty at eighteen when we first met.'

'Everyone is quite pretty at eighteen,' I retorted. 'A few decades later it is really quite enough to be clean and respectable, and I only hope I'm that. Anyway, I have no doubt that you would soon tell me if I weren't.'

Amy laughed, and began putting the clothes back among the tissue paper.

'Are you going away?' she asked.

'Not this holiday. At least, I haven't booked anything. I might slope off to Devon for a few days and hope to find bed and breakfast somewhere.'

'You'll be lucky! You really should organize yourself better. I'm always scolding you about it.'

'You are indeed,' I agreed, pouring her a glass of sherry.

'You know, even the *simplest* holiday needs to be arranged well in advance. James and I are having a few days in the Scillies at the end of next month, and we booked the hotel and the helicopter flight across from Penzance, way back in January.'

'Well, you're well-organized people, and I'm not.'

'With James so terribly busy we simply have to plan things, or we'd never get a break together. We propose to sleep, sunbathe, birdwatch and eat.'

'Sounds heavenly,' I said. 'I'll do it myself one day, when I can get round to arranging a holiday six months ahead.'

'I hope to live to see the day,' said Amy, putting down her empty glass. 'Well, I must be off. I'm glad you approve of my purchases.'

She looked rather sadly at my cardigan. 'How long have you had that shapeless garment?'

'About six years. And don't suggest that I give it to a jumble sale. It's pure wool, and hand-knitted by dear Mrs Willet. What's more, it's got *pockets*, which mighty few garments have these days, and I shall wear it till it drops into rags.'

'That won't be long!' Amy assured me, and drove off.

5. May

This is easily my favourite month and I greeted its arrival by remembering to say 'White Rabbits' aloud before uttering another syllable.

This childish superstition, told me first by a fellow six-year-old, is supposed to bring you luck for the rest of the month. When discussing such matters now, I tend to pooh-pooh the whole field of folklore, astrology, horoscopes and the rest of it, but I find myself hastily throwing spilt salt over my shoulder, dodging ladders and, if not in polite company, spitting in a ladylike way if I see one magpie.

Fortified by my 'White Rabbits' incantation, I got up and hung out of the bedroom window to relish the perfection of a May morning. The copper beech was in tiny leaf, which spread a rosy gauze over the tracery of bare branches. Dew shimmered on the grass, and drops of moisture on the hawthorn hedge sparked a hundred miniature rainbows.

Out in Mr Roberts's clover field a pheasant squawked. It was probably an anxious mother warning her chicks of the dangers that lurked around. Somewhere, high above, a lark was vying with another in the distance, the song pouring down from the blue in drops of pure music.

The air was cool, and deliciously scented with hyacinths and narcissi from the garden bed below. Later, it would be hot, and with luck I should be able to take my tea tray into the garden, after my day's work, and relish the joy of growing things. I remembered, with immense pleasure, that there was nothing in the diary for the evening of May the first. What bliss!

As I dressed, I pondered the problem of loneliness. I receive a great deal of unnecessary sympathy for my single state, and am touched by kind people's concern for the fact that I live alone. If they only knew! I find it much more exhausting to share my home with friends who come to stay, much as I love them, and the places I visit I remember much more clearly, and with keener affection, when I have visited them alone. I suppose that this is because one wanders around, looking at objects which are of particular personal interest, and absorbing their aspect and history without the distraction of a friend diverting one's attention to something which she has discovered.

No doubt, it tends to make one extremely selfish, but such solitude has its compensations. For one thing, it is possible to pursue a train of thought, or to carry out a piece of work, unmolested. I heartily sympathize with widows and widowers who are used to a shared life, and suffer horribly when that is shattered. The fact that so many of them adjust relatively quickly to the situation is indicative of their bravery; the fact that others never really recover is understandable. But, as a spinster, I have never been called upon to try to mend a broken life, and I am deeply grateful for that mercy. Amy's many attempts to marry me off have failed, I like to think, largely because of my contentment with my lot. It would be insupportable, of course, to think that the men were lukewarm!

The postman arrived as my egg was boiling. He brought a six-page document from the office about the necessity for Stringent Economies in Schools, and a glossy circular exhorting me to invest in a gold pendant which could be mine for rather more than two months' salary.

The latter went into the wastepaper basket, and the former I resigned myself to reading when I felt stronger.

But not this evening, I told myself, taking a refreshing look at the shimmering glory outside.

The first of May was going to be devoted to savouring its hope and beauty.

The Caxley Festival began to loom large. An enormous amount of organization had gone into its arrangements and *The Caxley Chronicle* carried copious advance notices of the pleasures in store and the absolute necessity of sending early for tickets, not forgetting the stamped addressed envelope for their return.

Although Fairacre was only on the edge of these stirring events and was spared the feverish activity in the market town itself, yet even so we had our small part in the excitement. The gardens, which were to be open on the first Saturday and Sunday of the month, were being tended with unnatural fervour. Mr Willet, whose garden is always in a state of perfection, was somewhat scathing about these unseemly efforts.

'There's no call for panic,' he told me, 'if you keeps the hoe going regular. Some of these people is going fair demented! Why, I heard as that new couple up the other end of the street, is planting out their geraniums, pots and all, from the greenhouse! Just to make a show! It's a scandal, I reckon, and if there's a sharp frost, as can often happen in May, they've lost the lot.' He puffed out his moustache in disgust, and moved off about his business.

Mrs Pringle was equally censorious when she arrived.

'Never saw so much fuss in all me borns,' she said, chins quivering. 'Did you know as Mr Mawne borrowed Mr Hales's electric shears to tidy up his yew hedge, and nearly killed hisself by cutting through the cable?'

I expressed my concern.

'Oh, he's come to no harm,' shrugged Mrs Pringle. 'But if he hadn't got into this fever it would never have happened. And they say the vicar's now worrying about people disturbing his new bees, and wishing he hadn't offered to open the garden at all. These 'ere festivals can cause a mint of trouble it seems.'

'They sometimes raise a mint of money,' I pointed out, and waited for the expected answer.

'As my dear mother used to say: "Money isn't –"'

Linda Moffat burst in upon Mrs Pringle's mother's well-known maxim to tell us that the youngest Coggs had locked himself in the lavatory and was yelling for help.

I went to supply it.

So often was my attention drawn to the Caxley Festival that I was not in the least surprised to hear Amy's voice on the telephone, and confidently awaited the news about some festival plans.

I was surprised to find that it was something entirely different that she had in mind.

'Am I right in thinking that in these decadent days you get a whole week's holiday around what, in our youth, was known as Whitsun?'

'That's right. Spring Bank Holiday is its official name, Amy, and it starts some time at the end of the month, and I believe we go back to school on Monday the third – maybe it's the fourth. I've mislaid my diary.'

'*Mislaid your diary?*' squeaked Amy, profoundly shocked. 'What on earth will you do?'

'It'll turn up,' I said vaguely. 'I may have chucked it into the wastepaper basket with some other rubbish, or I may have left it in the post office. I shall have a look today some time.'

'I have never met such a wholly lackadaisical person in my life,' scolded Amy. 'Why, if I were so careless as to lose my diary, I should be absolutely *daunted*! Life would have to stop until I'd found it again.'

'My life will tick over quite well without it for a day or two,' I assured her. 'What's the news?'

'Not very good, I'm afraid. James has muddled his dates, and now finds it is impossible for him to come to the Scillies at the end of the month. He has some engagement in Canada then, and we both wondered if you would like to come with me instead. What do you think? We were to go on the Sunday, stay overnight at Penzance, then fly across on the Monday morning. Do say you can come!'

'It sounds blissful! How long for?'

'We had planned to come back on the Thursday or Friday, so you'd have time to do any chores before school started again, if that's in your mind.'

I thought rapidly. I could not think of any particularly pressing engagement during that week, but without my diary it was difficult to be sure. I said as much to Amy, thanked her sincerely for an exciting invitation and promised to set about searching for my missing diary immediately.

'I'll ring you the minute it's found,' I assured her.

'And make the answer Yes,' said Amy, and rang off.

The first two or three days of May had been deliciously balmy, and we all told each other how lovely it would be if it lasted over the weekend.

Visions of suntanned visitors in summer frocks saunter-ing about the newly spruced Fairacre gardens kept most of us happy, but one or two pessimists shook their heads sadly. To my alarm, Mr Willet was one of them. He is such an accurate weather prophet that I viewed his forebodings seriously. The sky was cloudless on Friday afternoon and I only hoped that this time he might be wrong in his weather forecast.

But, sure enough, when I watched the weather man on television that evening, some ominous whirligigs, like well-spun spiders' webs, hovered unpleasantly near the west coast, and would bring rain and strong winds to the entire country. It was small comfort to learn that the weather would be more severe in the north than the south. The hardy types up there can take it, I thought callously, turning to our own dispiriting outlook which affected my feelings much more sharply.

I woke very early on Saturday morning. It was about five o'clock, and sure enough, a steady rain splashed along the gutters, and dripped from the trees. From the look of the garden, it had been pouring for several hours. Half a dozen sparrows splashed energetically in a large puddle by the box edging. The bird bath was full to the brim, though not being used for its right purpose by any of my bird friends.

The trees glistened, the roof tiles dropped miniature cascades on to those below, and some of the roses already drooped their heads, heavy with moisture. I decided to make myself a cup of tea and take it back to bed. Delicious Saturday morning, despite the rain, when I could call my time my own!

Tibby burst through the cat flap on the kitchen door, as I poured my tea, and rubbed her sopping-wet bedraggled body round my bare legs, ignoring my vituperation in an ecstasy of love. To salve my conscience, and to give myself time to get safely upstairs with my precious cup, I hastily put down some Pussi-luv, and hoped that she might mistake it for liver.

Hunched comfortably against the pillows I surveyed the streaming window over my cup. Would this rain stop? If not, would it be possible to postpone the opening of the gardens? And if so, how could it be advertised? I knew that a lot of people had planned to come from some distance to support the project. It was too bad.

I remembered that Irene Umbleditch and David Mawne were to be among our visitors, and looked forward to hearing their news. My mind went back to the time when David's unhappy little boy, Simon, spent a short time at Fairacre School. He would be away at boarding school now, and I wondered if we should ever meet again.

The rain continued all the morning, and by noon a nasty little wind had got up and was blowing the rain diagonally across the countryside. The sky was of uniform greyness. It was like being in a canvas tent, and the chances of a break in the clouds seemed non-existent.

The gardens were to be open from two o'clock until eight on both Saturday and Sunday, and I knew that several coachloads of people were expected from Caxley. At two o'clock, I donned wellingtons, my stoutest mackintosh and a rain hat which made me look like a witch, and set off bravely to do the rounds, or until exposure sent me home again.

It was heartening to see how many other people were doing the same. We met under umbrellas, in porches, under trees, anywhere to escape the relentless rain, and admired the dripping and battered beauty before us. A wonderful sense of camaraderie united us, as we sloshed our way around, and I was delighted to meet the Mawnes, their nephew and his bride-to-be, Irene, acting as hosts to the brave visitors in their garden.

They gave me good news of Simon.

'He's settled down very well now, and may move up next term. He's made friends with a pair of twins, two solid matter-of-fact youngsters who are marvellous ballast for our volatile Simon,' said David. 'We hope to take all three away in the summer, if their parents agree.'

Henry Mawne espied Miriam Quinn alone in the distance, and hurried to bring her over to meet his nephew. Once they were in conversation over a rare shrub of Henry's, I excused myself and splashed my way homeward.

To my surprise, the clock said four-thirty. It was no wonder I was wet. My expensive mackintosh had let water through the shoulders. My hair was plastered to my head by pressure from the ugly rain hat. My feet were soaked, as the rain had run down my legs into my wellingtons, but I was aglow with a sense of duty well done.

In this complacent and self-congratulatory state I decided to treat myself to a small fire on such a cheerless day. Whether the chimney was damp, which was understandable, or whether the wind was in the wrong direction, no one could say, but the result was unpleasant.

Clouds of acrid smoke blew into the room. My vision of 'the small but bright wood fire' beloved by novelists vanished in three minutes flat, as I set about opening windows, holding up newspapers over the fireplace to assist in the right sort of draught, and cursing generally whilst my smug feeling of virture rapidly evaporated.

Trust Fate to deflate one's ego!

The rain continued throughout the night. By morning, sheets of water covered the roads and some of Mr Roberts's fields. But slowly it improved, and by early afternoon a watery sun was visible fleetingly between the scudding clouds. It looked more hopeful for visitors to Fairacre's gardens, I thought.

Having done my duty the day before, I decided to do my ironing, polish my few pieces of silver, write some letters, and generally catch up with some long-neglected household jobs. But as I was about to switch on the iron, I saw that a bird was fluttering madly at one of the schoolroom windows.

I put down the iron, took the school key from its hook, and went to the rescue. As anyone who has been engaged on such an errand of mercy will know, the fact that every available window and door is open seems to make no

difference to the demented captive, which dashes itself wildly against all the closed apertures. After ten minutes' pandemonium the wretched sparrow darted out of the door, and I sank thankfully into my chair.

It was suddenly and blissfully peaceful. A shaft of watery sunshine illumined the classroom, a few dusty motes disturbed by the bird's and my agitation floating in its beam of light. A little breeze stirred one of the children's pictures pinned to the partition, but otherwise nothing ruffled the tranquillity of this ancient room.

It must be full of ghosts, I thought, or at least of memories. I found the idea comforting. How many children had sat in this place, imbibing knowledge both good and bad, observing the quirks of their neighbours, forming their own judgements, growing into the adult people they would be in a few years?

These same walls had seen the gamut of emotions from hilarity to despair. I remembered Miss Clare's remark about the celebratory tea party in the thirties, and the grief of children left fatherless in the First World War. This building had weathered sunshine and storm, peace and war. It had sheltered many who grew to be good men and women, and a few felons too. How far, I wondered, did the influence of this ancient school spread? All over the world there must be men and women who remembered something of the things taught them here, or were told of them by their forebears who knew the old school.

It came to me, with a poignancy I had not felt before, that I was an insignificant part of a worthy and long heritage. It was a humbling thought. Here was the heart of the matter, the spirit of the place, the unifying thread which ran through a hundred years. If only something of that spirit could be transmitted during our centenary celebrations!

I rose to return to my neglected kitchen tasks. As I

locked the school door, holding that same ancient key which had chilled the palms of so many of my predecessors, I thought with keener appreciation of the centenary story which was to be told. Would it be possible, I wondered, to express that feeling of continuity which had enveloped me in my silent schoolroom?

I had been busy with thoughts of Amy's kind invitation, and decided that I should love to go with her to Tresco in the week's holiday ahead. My diary turned up within ten minutes of our earlier conversation, but I had been unable to reach her on the telephone.

'I can only have been in the garden,' she assured me, when at last we made contact, 'and I can't tell you how glad I am you can come.'

'Not as glad as I am to have been invited. I've always wanted to see the Scillies, and never got round to it.'

'You won't be disappointed. Now, I think our best plan is for me to pick you up about eleven on the Sunday. We'll stop for a pub lunch, and then take our time getting to Penzance. We should be there in good time for a nice dinner. We're booked in at the Queen's, and the food is always good.'

'Perfect,' I said.

'Have you found that diary?'

'Of course I have!'

'No "of course!" about it,' said Amy severely. 'But put down these arrangements while you remember them.'

'I'm not *quite* senile,' I protested.

'And don't forget my poetry reading on Wednesday. I'm counting on you to lead the clapping.'

'I'll be there,' I promised her, and we rang off.

But Fate decreed otherwise.

A week or so earlier, a sizeable chunk of stopping had

dropped out of a back tooth. As it had not hurt, and I already had an appointment with the dentist within a month, I had ignored the gaping hole, except for wiggling at it with my tongue now and again.

Wednesday's school dinner consisted of rissoles, mashed potato and peas, followed by a sticky treacle tart which was welcomed rapturously by the children. Without thinking, I tackled my slice, only to be smitten with the most piercing pain in my damaged tooth.

I was obliged to leave the children to Miss Briggs's care and rush to the schoolhouse for first aid. The oil of cloves bottle, well hidden behind cough mixture, alka seltzer, aspirin tablets, and a particularly sinister bottle labelled 'The Mixture' – for what malady I had completely forgotten – was found to have about two drops of thickened syrup at the bottom which I did my best to apply with a wooden cherry stick wrapped in cotton wool.

If anything, this treatment seemed to aggravate the pain, and I hastily mixed a solution of my old friend TCP with warm water and tried again. But this time the pain was throbbing in my ear as well. By dint of holding warm TCP solution in my mouth, a slight diminution of pain resulted, but it was obvious that I could not take a class with my mouth bulging with water.

I tottered back just in time to see Mrs Pringle arriving for the washing up.

'Why, you do look bad!' she greeted me, with much satisfaction. 'You mark my words, that face'll be up like a plum pudden in an hour or two. You wants to tie a stocking round your jaw, and my auntie in Caxley always swore by some mustard in the tooth to keep it warm.'

I felt unequal to replying, and watched Mrs Pringle make for the lobby with a heavy limp. This was a sure sign that she was affronted, had taken umbrage, and was in her martyred mood. By this time, my tooth hurt so much that I was beyond caring if Mrs Pringle slit her throat with one of the school knives, although she would have had to be pretty determined in the face of such uncooperative bluntness.

I stuck it out until playtime when I confessed my plight to Miss Briggs, who proved sympathetic and willing to cope with the school for the rest of the afternoon, while I returned to the schoolhouse and rang the dentist.

'Aren't you lucky?' said his receptionist, and while I was recovering from this remark, she added, 'We've just had a cancellation. If you can get here by a quarter to five, Mr Bennett will see you then.'

Kind Mr Bennett! Dear Mr Bennett, I thought gratefully! I was positively longing to see him. Usually the thought of going to the dentist – even one as humane as Mr Bennett – casts a gloom over my life for days ahead. Now, crazed with pain, even with a mouthful of hot TCP, I viewed my trip to Caxley as a drowning man must view a lifeboat.

I went across the playground to apprise Miss Briggs of events and to lock up my cupboards and desk. The children were blissfully quiet, as they usually are in a crisis. The dividing door was propped open, so that the infants' teacher could keep an eye on them, and I returned to get wrapped up when I remembered Amy's party.

There was nothing for it but to cry off. In my present state, I could not have sat through a commercial television jingle, let alone two or three hours of Caxley culture. Amy was wholeheartedly sympathetic, and magnanimous about my defection.

'You poor old darling! Take as many painkillers as you can, and a warm bath, and crawl into bed as soon as you get back. I'll ring tomorrow to see how you are, and tell you how it went tonight. Now, tie something round your face before you venture out, or you'll have earache as well.'

'I have already. And Mrs Pringle suggests a stocking.'

'Mrs Pringle is a fool!' said Amy forcefully. 'Nylon's useless. You want a silk scarf.'

Wonderfully cheered by hearing Mrs Pringle denounced in such a forthright manner, I rang off, and went upstairs to swathe myself as directed.

I fairly galloped into Mr Bennett's presence when summoned. He looked astounded at the speed with which I clambered into the dreaded chair and displayed my raging tooth. Usually he is obliged to lead me to the seat murmuring soothing noises as grooms do to nervous horses.

'We'll soon settle that,' he said. 'Just temporarily, of course. I'll give you a shot, and a temporary filling, and we'll make an appointment to do the job properly when the inflammation has gone.'

I surrendered myself to his ministrations with only an occasional yelp and whimper, and was home again within half an hour.

I took Amy's advice and went to bed. Tibby followed me, and we snuggled down together, the cat on top, pinning the bed clothes down uncomfortably, but I was past worrying.

It was bliss to be in bed before six o'clock, and comparatively free from pain. My final thought was of Amy's concert, and all the hard work she had put into providing a successful evening. What a broken reed I was!

Nevertheless, despite my guilt, I fell asleep within minutes, and only surfaced when the alarm clock called me to face another day.

Amy was as good as her word and rang me after school the next day. After kind enquiries about my temporarily quiescent tooth, she told me that the evening had been a huge success.

'And you were *much* missed,' she added. 'Everyone enquiring after you and desolated to hear about the tooth-ache. Do you know, we made nearly sixty pounds?'

'Marvellous,' I said, suitably impressed.

'Including the raffle, of course, and some records Jean Cole sent as she couldn't come herself. And the food seemed to suit everybody.'

'I bet it did, knowing your usual efforts.'

'Do you know, there were some veal patties left and Tim Ferdinand asked if he could have them to take home! What a strange man he is! Not that I minded. He's so emaciated I was glad to provide tonight's supper as well as yesterday's, but I must say I felt that I was making up a doggie bag as I packed the remnants.'

'It's probably because he's a poet. His standards of behaviour are quite different from normal, no doubt.'

'Yes, well, there it is. The veal patties have found a kind home evidently. For two pins I believe he would have taken the dregs of wine too. He was looking rather keenly at the bottles as he left.'

Amy reminded me about our holiday plans. I promised to be ready in good time, and we exchanged farewells.

The few days before that longed-for holiday were spent in reading-tests, a school medical inspection, patching up my tooth, and in writing a letter to the office pointing out that work on the skylight had still not begun, and why not?

But on Friday we broke up, and Sunday morning dawned clear and bright. Here was May at its best, and I carried my case downstairs with a glad heart.

Amy was punctual, refused coffee, complimented me upon my neat appearance, and we set off westward. After ten minutes' secret anxiety about whether I had switched off everything switchable, whether I had left out the tin-opener for Tibby's Pussi-luv which Mrs Pringle was kindly giving her, and whether I had shut the pantry window

which usually gets forgotten, I gave myself up to the
enjoyment of the drive. Time enough to worry if I returned
to a smoking ruin, I told myself, looking resolutely
through the side window.

There was comparatively little traffic, and in any case
Amy is an excellent driver. The green hedges streamed
past, sprinkled here and there with curds of white May
blossom. Cows stood knee deep in lush meadows, the
sunshine gleaming on their glossy coats. The heat shimmered on Salisbury Plain. The distant hills were smudges
of blue in the clear atmosphere, and the sun grew hotter as
we sped on.

We stopped for lunch, and again later in the afternoon to
have a walk. The lane where we drew off ran deep between
steep banks. Primroses were still out on the shady side, and
young bracken and hart's tongue fern delighted us both.
Through a gateway we saw a little stream far below us, and
on a tree stump a humped bird.

'Look!' whispered Amy, and even as she grabbed my
arm, the bird spread its wings and dived towards the water
– a vivid flash of pink and blue.

'A kingfisher!' we cried together.

'That means good luck,' Amy told me, as we set off to
the car to resume our trip.

We reached Penzance soon after tea, wandered round
the town, ate an admirable dinner, and slept like tops.

The helicopter journey across to St Mary's the next
morning was exciting. Below us the farms and trees looked
like the models which my children so enjoy setting out, and
between the islands the sea glinted in the sunshine, green
and blue, with creamy surf lashing the rocks. I wished the
journey could have lasted longer. One saw so much, at just
the right height it seemed to me, and I looked forward to
the return journey.

We took a boat from St Mary's to Tresco, and were soon

settled in our hotel. Hanging out of the bedroom window, I surveyed the scene.

The light was wonderful, pellucid and luminous. It reminded me of the light Amy and I had rejoiced in when we spent a holiday in Crete together some years earlier. Perhaps all islands have this peculiar quality, a reflection, maybe, of the water around them.

The sea was as vivid a blue as the kingfisher's flashing wings, and toppled lazily upon white sandy beaches which I had only seen before in holiday brochures. Gorse blazed yellow near by, and the accumulation of dazzling colours was heady stuff indeed.

Amy entered the room as I gazed, entranced.

'I think I could settle here for ever,' I told her.

'It can be pretty windy,' she warned me. 'You've only seen its fair-weather face.'

'It can be pretty windy at Fairacre,' I retorted, 'and not half as beautiful.'

'Wait until you've seen the rest,' said Amy. 'There's plenty to fall in love with.'

As usual, she was right. Everyone told us how lucky we were with the weather, for the sun shone for every day of our short stay, and we were able to quarter the island of Tresco on foot and visit the miraculous Abbey Gardens.

Sometimes we took a boat to one of the neighbouring islands, and Amy, who is almost as knowledgeable about birds as Henry Mawne, was thrilled to study all sorts of rare varieties at St Agnes through her field glasses.

I was far less energetic, being quite content to soak up the wonderful sunshine and sea air, and to give admiring grunts when Amy told me about such wonders as rock thrushes and buntings and kittiwakes and divers she was observing with rapture.

The days passed all too swiftly. As our boat chugged

away from Tresco and its white sands, I promised myself another visit before I was too old and decrepit to enjoy tramping round its beautiful bays.

On our long drive back I tried to tell Amy how much I had appreciated the holiday, and how perfect she was as a companion and guide.

She patted my knee.

'You do me good,' she said, and then went on to say the most surprising things.

'I envy you, you know, teaching away at Fairacre, always busy, knowing where you are going, seeing progress with those lucky children of yours. I seem to lead such a *useless* sort of life.'

'I've never heard such rubbish,' I protested. 'Why, you run that house perfectly, and look after James, and still find time for all sorts of good works, like that poetry evening, for instance. What's more, you look a dream always and are a delight to everyone's eye.'

'Well, thank you, my dear. I'm grateful, but the truth is, it's not enough. I can do all those things quite easily, I suppose, and so do thousands of other ordinary women like me, but I should like to do something which is especially *me*! I used to paint passably, but I know I shall never be much good at it. I wondered – don't laugh at me – but do you think I could *possibly* write my autobiography?'

'I know you could. And very well too. When are you starting?'

Amy laughed, and the tension was broken. 'Lord knows! I expect I shall be one of those people who is constantly saying she is going to write a book "when she can find the time". Lucy Clayton is one of them.'

Lucy Clayton was at college when we were, and I found her insufferable. Amy sees her occasionally, while I try to avoid her.

'Lucy Clayton,' I said, 'is incapable of *speaking* the

Queen's English let alone *writing* it. But you carry on, Amy. I'll see you keep at it, and I promise to buy the first copy.'

'You are very encouraging,' said Amy. 'As good as a tonic.'

'Or a holiday in the Scillies, maybe? Do you know, Amy, we shall be home in less than an hour, and for once in my life I shall have mixed feelings about being in Fairacre again.'

6. June

Of course, when it came to it, I slipped back into my usual routine within hours, and the glories of the Scillies seemed just a happy dream. A surprising number of people commented on my improved appearance.

'You was looking a bit peaky,' Mr Willet told me. 'I said to the missus a way back, "Miss Read looks proper poorly," but now, well, you looks as hearty as my old porker in his sty!'

Mrs Pringle's description was even more impressive.

'They've fattened you up a treat. You looked like a ghost before you had that holiday – real white and spiteful, if you know what I mean.'

I replied civilly that I was glad to know that I looked better. Privately I wondered what on earth I must have looked like to have been described as 'proper poorly', 'white and spiteful' and even now – after my metamorphosis – as 'a porker'. Ah well! At least vanity would not be added to my array of sins.

'See *The Caxley* since you've been back?' asked Mrs Pringle. I translated this as meaning *The Caxley Chronicle*. The phrase *The Caxley* can cover one or two objects, such as the local bus to the market town. I have heard people say, 'You'll have to catch *The Caxley* and then change.'

I admitted that I had not yet looked at the paper.

'It's got Mrs Benson's house in it this week. Nice place it looks – bigger than it is really. Something to do with the way they tilts the camera no doubt.'

'We shall all miss her,' I said.

'The worst of it is, it don't give no price,' said Mrs Pringle gloomily. 'I do like to see how much people has the nerve to ask these days. Looks as though it's going to be auctioned. I suppose these 'ere estate agents hopes people will be carried away and offer more than it's worth. I remember my brother-in-law going crazy at one sale and buying a piece of stair carpet for three pounds.'

'That sounds quite a bargain to me.'

'Not when you had to lug away a broken fireguard, one of them exercising bicycles, a zinc bath and four chamber pots, if you'll excuse my mentioning them.'

'Not at all,' I said graciously.

'My sister fairly gave him a taste of her tongue, for all she belongs to the Plymouth Brethren. They had to pay Percy Potter another pound for bringing the stuff home on his carrier's van, and of course all the neighbours fell about laughing and making coarse remarks when the stuff came up the front path. No, my brother-in-law never heard the last of that, I can tell you!'

Mrs Pringle heaved herself from the front desk where she had been resting, and made for the stove. A dead leaf was sullying its summer perfection, and Mrs Pringle removed it with as much venom as she would have displayed if it had been a tarantula spider.

Later that day I looked up the advertisement. Holly Lodge certainly made an attractive picture, and the accommodation sounded ideal.

'Too big for us,' I told Tibby, 'and too expensive. But I hope some nice family comes to enjoy it.'

'The property includes a self-contained flat comprising a large sitting room, bedroom, bath and kitchen, on the ground floor, all in immaculate condition.'

Poor Miss Quinn, I thought! How she will hate leaving her flat, all in immaculate condition! I knew how happy she had been in Joan Benson's company. As Fairacre folk had said truly, it would not be easy for her to find such a home elsewhere.

And although I only knew Miriam Quinn slightly, I should be sorry to see her go from Fairacre. I liked her quiet contentment, the tranquil exterior which hid, I suspected, a power house of energy.

She obviously loved Fairacre, her solitude and her uninterrupted thoughts.

We had a lot in common.

During our stay in Tresco I had tried to tell Amy something of the feelings which had stirred me that afternoon alone in the schoolroom. Was it possible, I asked her, to put across such a theme in our centenary celebrations?

Amy was thoughtful for a time, and then said that she doubted if it would be possible.

'It's something purely evocative,' she said. 'I'm quite sure that lots of people in Fairacre feel the same way about their old school, but to express it, especially through the children who are the agents in this case, is well-nigh impossible, I think.

'You'll have to be content with coming down to a more earthy approach. Your idea of various happenings during the hundred years seems far more practical, and incidentally will show the continuity you are aiming at. Play for simplicity, is my advice.'

I was sure Amy was right, the more I thought about it. Anything verging on the high-falutin' could prove boring or sentimental.

I asked Miss Briggs to stay to tea one afternoon, and we set about tackling the programme. Not that our surroundings were conducive to heavy thought. The pinks in my border were beginning to shake out their shaggy heads, and the crimson feathers of peony petals fluttered to the baked earth beneath.

We sat in the shade of my old plum tree, tea cups in hand, and relished the peace of a June afternoon. In the distance we could hear the steady thumping of a baler. Someone had cut an early crop of hay, it seemed. A blackbird scurried among the plants in the dry border, searching for titbits for its young family, and overhead our ever-present downland larks kept up their fervent outpouring.

'Well, I suppose we'd better make a start,' I said at last. I could easily have drifted into sleep in these soporific surroundings, but it was hardly a good example to my assistant.

'Are you thinking of ten scenes, one for each decade,' asked Miss Briggs with unusual briskness, 'or a scene for each reign?'

'I hadn't really decided that point,' I admitted.

'And we shall have to have a narrator, of course. You'd better do that.'

I began to feel some awe for Miss Briggs. Who would have imagined she would be quite so efficient?

'I had dallied with the idea of one of the children doing that,' I replied.

'Oh, I think the thing needs to be held together by someone with authority,' said Miss Briggs. 'Besides, none of the children really reads well enough, and all of them are bound to be nervous in front of an audience.'

I did not like to say that I should be nervous myself, but agreed meekly that it might be a good idea for me to do the linking. 'But not much of it,' I added. 'Just a few sentences to show what is happening in the world outside, and then a true scene straight from the log book.'

'And what about music?'

'Oh, heavens above,' I groaned. My piano playing is minimal, and Miss Briggs's non-existent. We could have records, I supposed?

'Well, we'll think about that,' said my assistant, now

busily making notes on a pad. 'But some singing might go down well, if we can get an accompanist. After all, that piano of ours has been here since the school started. It ought to have a part in the performance.'

We worked for an hour or more as the teapot cooled in the grass at our feet, and a few early gnats hovered around. By that time, we had decided that the next step was to ransack the log book for suitable scenes, with not too many players in them, and to use the whole school as a chorus whenever it could be incorporated.

'Must let the mums see their offspring in the limelight,' remarked Miss Briggs sagaciously. 'It's half the battle.'

With that, we carried in our tea things and I saw the lady off, feeling more respect for my partner than ever before.

As all Fairacre had foreseen, work began on the skylight some two months later than planned, and it was quite clear that the rest of the summer term would pass to the accompaniment of loud noises above, and showers of a century's rubbish falling about us.

To give Reg Thorn his due, he certainly apologized very prettily. No doubt he got plenty of practice, was my private tart comment. He also rigged up a tarpaulin just under the skylight which was intended to catch the bits, but also blocked a great deal of light. I had not realized how much we relied on this ancient window for illumination until the tarpaulin flapped above my desk.

It was all very annoying, and of course the children's attention was more distracted than ever. Reg Thorn appeared himself for the first hour or so each day, and then left his two younger assistants to carry on.

'Got quite a lot of other jobs on hand,' he explained. 'Got some shelving for the Mawnes, and a little job at Beech Green. If I keep an eye on them it keeps you all happy.'

I should like to have pointed out that finishing one job satisfactorily and then proceeding to the next on the date given originally and staying there till *that* job was done, would make us all a great deal happier. But before I could voice these sentiments Reg Thorn had departed. Such expert slipping away could also be the result of years of experience, I thought to myself.

Later in the morning, when we were about to clear the desks ready for school dinner, Eileen Burton rushed in from the lobby in a state of panic.

'There's a funny man in the playground,' she gasped.

At once there was a rush to the door. The mob checked there and turned to me in some dismay.

'He's all dressed up in white, miss.'

'Got one of them sun 'ats on, miss.'

'He's blowing smoke, miss.'

'Looks like a man from Mars to me, miss,' said the school wag.

'Well, let me come through and then I can see,' I said. A narrow passage was made through the milling mass.

Sure enough, a white-clad figure, crowned with a topee from which white veiling fell to the shoulders, roamed apparently aimlessly round the playground. In its hand was a contraption with a nozzle which occasionally belched blue smoke. Memories of a recent television programme, which I had been too idle to switch off, came back to me.

'It's the vicar,' I told them.

'He'd never dress up all funny,' Ernest rebuked me.

'Looking for bees,' I continued. 'Now go inside, and I'll have a word with him.'

Reluctantly they moved back a few feet. I did not imagine for a moment that they would return to their desks. Curiosity was too strong for them, but at least they stayed in the safety of the lobby and watched the proceedings.

I was within touching distance of our vicar before he became aware of me, so engrossed was he in surveying the hedges and trees which border the playground.

'Oh, my dear Miss Read,' he exclaimed. 'How you startled me!'

I expressed my regret.

'I should have let you know that I was coming, but time pressed. Mr Lamb rang to say a swarm of bees was passing over – he thought they might be mine – so of course I got my things together, and ventured out.'

He compressed the bellows of the gadget in his hand and smoke issued forth.

'My smoker,' he said, with pride. 'It's still working, thank heaven. It calms the bees so that you can drop them into the skep easily.'

He nodded towards the school wall where a fine straw skep awaited the elusive swarm.

'But surely, they might be miles away,' I said. At that moment, Mrs Partridge's face peered over the wall which divides the school playground from the vicar's garden.

'Gerald! Gerald! Margaret Waters has just rung to say the bees are in her damson tree, and could you come quickly before they get into the chimney.'

'Into the chimney?' echoed the vicar in amazement. 'Why on earth should they wish to go into a *chimney* when they can enjoy the sunshine and fresh air on a damson tree?'

'I don't know the *reason*, Gerald,' said Mrs Partridge, sounding justifiably exasperated, 'I am simply repeating her message – so *hurry*!'

The vicar obediently collected his skep, threw back the veil from his perspiring countenance, and set off on his errand of mercy.

Later, Mr Willet spoke of the episode.

'D'you see the vicar in his moonship gear this morning? My word, he fair set all the village dogs barking their heads off as he went by! And young Mrs Smith's baby was outside in his pram, and hasn't stopped bawling since.'

'But did he take the swarm?' I asked.

'Oh, he took 'em all right,' said Mr Willet off-handedly. 'They're in the skep in the shade. Miss Waters said the vicar's coming to get them at dusk. But just to be on the safe side she told Mr Mawne, and he's promised to help collect 'em. He's a better man than I am, Gunga Din,' said Mr Willet, misquoting Kipling. 'I wouldn't go near a swarm of bees for all the tea in China. Did I ever tell you about my old gran's?'

'Yes,' I said, and went to pick up an infant who had fallen painfully and deservedly from the coke pile.

There was an agreeable literary sequel to this adventure. When the vicar called to bring in the hymn list at the end of the week, I naturally enquired after the bees.

'It was an extraordinary thing,' said the vicar. 'Henry and I collected the skep during the evening, and he helped me to transfer it to an old hive he lent me. But do you know, they simply would not stay in it! Luckily, I had a new hive not in use, so later we transferred them to that one, and since then we've had no trouble.'

'What was wrong with Henry's hive, do you think?'

'I think dear old Parson Woodforde put his finger on it some two hundred years ago. You know his diary, I have no doubt?'

I very nearly said it was my Bible, but remembering to whom I was speaking, hastily said it was a great favourite of mine.

'I looked up the passage, and he says something to the effect that he too had to hive a swarm twice. The first hive had evidently been kept in a barn and he suspected that mice or other small animals had used it. I liked his final comment that: "Bees are particularly Nice and Cleanly." He must have been a singularly kind and observant man, and obviously loved his bees.'

Such a warm smile illumined the cherubic countenance of our own parson, that I thought he shared many of Parson Woodforde's virtues.

The Caxley Spring Festival had netted over a thousand pounds, the local paper informed us, and more was expected as one or two extra efforts were still to be held. One of these was a flower festival involving half a dozen beautifully decked churches, St Patrick's being one of them.

I wandered in one evening to admire the exquisite arrangements. To my mind every one was perfect, a miracle of form and fragrance. It astonished me to hear the comments of two women who were following me round the display. They were evidently keen flower arrangers and knew all the things one should be looking for.

'My dear,' said one, 'just *look* at that pedestal! One can positively see the Oasis!'

'Dreadful,' agreed her friend, with a shudder, 'and she has obviously *never heard* of the Hogarth line!'

I only hoped that the arranger was not within earshot.

When I emerged from the church into the golden evening, a woman hailed me. Her name, luckily, I remembered. She was a Mrs Austen, and once belonged to our Women's Institute. We had not seen each other for months, and we greeted each other enthusiastically.

As she had seen the flowers and had time to spare, she came back to the schoolhouse with me.

'We're at Springbourne now,' she told me. 'My husband had the chance of a job in London, but we wouldn't take it although the money was better. We've been countrymen ever since we were evacuated.'

'Tell me more,' I begged her. 'Were you at Fairacre School? You know it's our centenary this year?'

'Yes, I was, and no, I didn't know,' she replied. 'I came down right at the beginning of the war. We lived in Camberwell in south London, and pretty crowded we were in our flat. There were three of us children. I was the youngest, just six when war broke out. We'd all been to the big L.C.C. school round the corner, and a very good grounding we got there.

'Mind you, the classes were big – over fifty of us altogether, and the teachers had to keep order pretty well or nothing would have been learnt. Looking back, we did a lot of class work the children today wouldn't like. Chanting tables, and reading round the class out of the same reader, that sort of thing. And no end of spelling tests and mental arithmetic, all done very fast, and devil take the hindmost.'

'But you got on, obviously.'

'Oh, we all got on. In those days the teachers were the best in the country, we were told. They got the highest salaries, so the committee could take the pick of the training colleges when they appointed staff. They certainly made us work. I think that's partly why I liked Fairacre so much. The pace was slower and the teachers were quieter.'

'Was that all you liked? It must have been an upheaval to be evacuated.'

She shook her head. 'I told you we were crowded at home, and at school. Mine was a very respectable family. Mother kept us all spotless, and the house was polished to the nines. But we only had one room really to live in comfortably – the front room – and that was turned into a bedroom at night for my two brothers.

'Behind that was the kitchen, and it was always so dark that we had to have the gas burning. And behind that was the only bedroom, where I slept on a little truckle-bed next to my parents.'

'Any garden?'

'Just a tiny paved yard where Mother hung her washing. If we wanted to see grass we had to be taken to the park. We weren't allowed to go on our own, because the roads were too busy.'

'So all these fields seemed wonderful?'

'Do you know, when we got out at Caxley Station and stood in lines with our little cardboard boxes holding our gas masks, some of the children were crying. But not me! There were lovely grassy banks, and roses in flower, and the air was just beautiful. I felt I had come home.'

'And that feeling stayed?'

'It's never gone away! As we drove to Fairacre with our new foster parents I grew happier and happier. Of course, I missed my father and mother, and at night-time, if I woke, I sometimes wept a bit for them. But Fairacre was bliss to me, and the children were kind to us as well as the teachers.'

'I'm glad to hear it.'

'We all squashed up together in the desks. Two of our teachers had come with us, nice lively girls they were. It couldn't have been easy for anyone, because every scrap of space was used, and we even had a couple of classes in the village hall. But after a bit, a lot of the children drifted back to London as there weren't any raids, so things settled down very comfortably. Mr Fortescue was the head-master, and Miss Clare was teaching here then. How is she?'

I gave her news of our old friend.

'If ever there was a saint, she's one,' said Mrs Austen. 'I suppose she's coming to the celebrations?'

'I hope she'll tell us some of her memories,' I replied. 'She knows more about Fairacre School than anyone living.'

'She helped us all to settle in,' remembered Mrs Austen. 'You know there were a lot of things that shook us about the country. Cows for one, and earth closets for another. And I was scared stiff of real darkness in a winter's lane, after lamp posts along the pavements. I think our hostesses had plenty to put up with. On the whole I like to think that we three didn't give too much trouble. We'd been brought up quite strictly, and my parents came down at least twice a month, and made sure we behaved properly. But there were some pretty rough families, as you can guess, and all that talk about bed-wetting and head lice and impetigo and scabies and so on – well, a lot of it was true.'

'We get the odd case now,' I told her. 'Fairacre isn't unadulterated Arcady, you know.'

'I realize that, but to me as a six-year-old Fairacre *was* Arcady, and this part of England has stayed that way, to my mind, ever since.'

'I'm inclined to agree,' I said.

Mrs Pringle arrived the next morning looking full of importance, and with no trace of a limp. She had the appearance of one with a message to deliver.

It was sad news.

'Bob Willet says he won't be in today until later. His poor brother Sid has passed on, and Bob's gone over there to see his sister-in-law and fix up the funeral.'

I murmured condolences.

'Well, he's been bad for months, poor soul. Something to do with his digestion – the *lower* end of it, if you know what I mean. I never liked to ask Bob too much about it, as it was rather a *personal* complaint.'

'Aren't they all?'

'Some,' said Mrs Pringle frostily, 'is more personal than others.' And she swept away.

Mr Willet looked rather subdued when he appeared in the late afternoon, and shook his head sadly when I expressed my sorrow.

'Thank God I didn't have to see him dead,' he said. 'Never let anyone show you a corpse, specially if you've been fond of the person. My mum made me kiss my grandma in her coffin, and I've never got over it. What's more, I can never remember my gran as she was when she was alive. The look of her dead face is the only one I can see. A pity! She was a lively old party and I loved her a lot.'

I said I'd heard about her from several of her Fairacre friends.

'She was good to us kids. There was five of us, and not much money, of course. We lived in a cottage at Springbourne and my gran lived near by. We always called in going to and from school, and she used to put an apple or some plums in our dinner basket.

'Sid was the eldest. He was quite a scholar, used to sit there when old Hope was headmaster,' Mr Willet nodded towards a corner desk at the back. 'He could have gone to the grammar school, but with all of us to keep Dad said he'd best get out working. Old Sid never complained and he made a durn fine cabinet maker in the end, but I reckon he minded a bit about not going to Caxley Grammar.'

Mr Willet sighed, and began to make for the door. 'It's a funny thing, when someone dies, you never remember them as they were then, but always as children. I saw poor old Sid in hospital last week, but all I can see now is Sid about ten, lugging the rush basket with our school dinners up the hill here to Fairacre School. Or swinging our little sister round and round by her hands, or feeding his pet rabbit.'

He opened the schoolroom door. 'Old Sid will always be about ten for me. Funny really!'

'Perhaps that's as it should be,' I told him.

When I saw Amy next I repeated Mr Willet's remarks about viewing the dead.

'It's perfectly true,' she agreed. 'I can't say I've seen many dead people, but the two aunts whose bodies I saw simply will not come to life for me now. I always do my best *not* to see corpses for that reason. I like to remember my relatives as they were.'

'I'm remarkably short of close relatives,' I said, 'though I'm told I look more and more like my Aunt Bessie the older I grow. I'm sorry to say she was remarkably plain, but very determined.'

'I often wonder if we only see the *good* points of relatives in ourselves. You say your Aunt Bessie was *determined*. Maybe she was just pig-headed. I know I like to think I have my Aunt Maud's efficiency, but really I know she was plain *bossy*, and nearly drove poor Uncle Edward demented. She would tidy away his jigsaw puzzle and put it back in the box when he was only halfway through.'

'Strong grounds for divorce,' I said. 'Have some coffee?' And we went into the kitchen together to make it.

7. July

Speculation about Holly Lodge grew keener as the weeks passed. The preliminary announcement of its sale by auction, 'unless sold privately beforehand', whetted all appetites.

Mrs Pringle had heard from an unspecified source, but she told me it was as true as she stood there, that nothing under fifty thousand pounds would be considered. Mr Willet observed that people must need their heads examined when it came to buying houses these days, and Reg Thorn said he could remember when Holly Lodge belonged to that miserable old faggot that drove a Liverpool phaeton. His name was on the tip of his tongue, but he reckoned it had gone for the moment. Anyway, when he had died – and no one mourned his going, that was a fact – Holly Lodge went for six hundred to a nice old party from the other side of Caxley. Six hundred, mark you!

Later in the morning, he drew aside the tarpaulin, sending a shower of dried paint and wood splinters upon us, poked his face through the gap, and said:

'Potter! That was the name! Josiah Potter, and a nasty bit of work he was too.'

He then withdrew, allowing me to send Ernest out to the lobby for the dustpan and brush, whilst I continued my interrupted discourse on medieval farming methods.

The sale of Holly Lodge occupied the inhabitants of Fairacre very pleasurably. The history of the house, the quirks of its various owners and, of course, the scandalous amount of money being asked for it at the moment, were all mulled over with the greatest enjoyment.

Whether any would-be purchasers had inspected the house was difficult to say. Holly Lodge was a little distance from the centre of the village and well hidden from prying eyes by the high hedge which gave the house its name. It was one of Fairacre's more retired establishments, and as Mrs Pringle remarked wistfully: 'It's difficult to find out what goes on in there.'

It so happened that I met Miriam Quinn and Joan Benson on separate occasions within a week. I had gone into Caxley on one sunny Saturday morning to buy a pair of summer shoes, and was still reeling from the shock of the amount I had just handed over, when I bumped into Miriam Quinn.

She commiserated with me.

'I can sympathize. I've just come from inspecting cotton frocks, and have decided that my present shabby collection can do another year – if not two or three.'

I asked after Joan.

'Run off her feet at the moment, with people coming to view. She won't have any difficulty in disposing of it, I'm sure, but she does so want to see it in good hands. Half the viewers have appalling plans for turning it into flats, or a home for delinquent boys or some such.'

I said that it must be a trying time for them both.

'Well, there it is. I haven't found anything remotely suitable for myself, and I'm now at the limbo stage, telling myself I may as well wait and see, and perhaps something will turn up. Somehow one gets numb after a bit.'

'Maybe that's nature's protection,' I said, as we parted.

Joan Benson I met in the village a day or two later. She was struggling with an overloaded carrier bag which had collapsed under the strain, and only had one handle intact.

'I really should have brought the car, but I thought it would do me good to walk on such a heavenly day. In any case, I only intended to buy about four things, and now look at me!'

'Here, put some in my basket, and come back with me and I'll let you have a good tough bag. I'm going to have a cup of tea anyway, so do join me.'

The children had gone home, and I had been to the post office to send off a couple of urgent missives to the office, which would probably not be opened for days, if I knew anything about it.

Over tea, Joan told me more about the horrors of selling a home. 'I don't know which is worse – trying to find a home, or trying to get rid of one. For two pins, I'd call the whole thing off and just stay at Holly Lodge until I'm carried out feet first.'

'There would be general rejoicing if you did decide to stay,' I told her.

'Well, that's nice to hear, but I really must be sensible and look ahead. This wretched arthritis gets steadily more troublesome, and sometimes I find it quite difficult to get upstairs. And the house is far too big now that I'm alone, and costs the earth to heat. And much as I love gardening, I simply cannot cope with that great one at Holly Lodge, and help gets more and more impossible to find, and more and more expensive.'

She sighed, and shook her head at the proffered biscuit tin.

'What a misery I sound! I'm not really unhappy, I've been so kindly looked after in Fairacre I shall miss the life here horribly. But my daughter is quite right. If I can't drive, I shall be absolutely done for in Fairacre, and I'm finding it quite painful sometimes. And I'm sorry to say that I am now refusing to drive at night, or if it's foggy or icy.'

'That cuts it down quite considerably,' I agreed, and she laughed.

'But it's selling the house which is the real problem. I don't want Miriam to have to go. She's been quite wonderful to me, and is so happily ensconced in that little annexe. If only we could find a nice quiet family that would be glad to have her there, and people that Miriam could get on with, it would be perfect. But that means selling to someone we know, and so far no one in that category has emerged. And some of the viewers have fairly curdled my blood with their plans for the house!'

'They probably wouldn't get them passed anyway when it came to the point.'

'But I *love* that house,' cried Joan. 'I simply hate the idea of it being torn about. If only some nice couple who like it as it is would appear, I should sell cheerfully. As it is, I still have to find myself somewhere near Barbara. She is quite marvellous about vetting places, but with young children she is very tied, and I feel I must go and stay with her before long to have a good scout round myself.'

She began to collect her shopping.

'I've run on far too long, but you are so sympathetic. And thank you for the delicious tea, and the bag, and best of all for *listening*.'

On the doorstep she paused.

'You won't mention my concern about Miriam, will you? I should hate her to think I was turning buyers away because of her. It's not *quite* like that, as I'm sure you understand, but she is so independent . . .'

Her voice trailed away.

'Never fear,' I assured her. 'I've lived in a village long enough to know how to be discreet. Though even then, it's sometimes difficult to keep the boat up straight.'

She waved, and departed with her burden.

Mr Lamb at the post office unearthed a handful of ancient postcards from the back of a little-used drawer. He came across one of Fairacre School which he kindly gave me, and I pored over it with a magnifying glass.

This photograph must have been taken in the first decade of this century, judging by the dress of the children. They are all gathered in the lane outside the school and there is not a single piece of traffic in sight.

How instantly that picture carried me into a vanished world! The boys are grouped together on one side of the lane, and every one of them wears a cap. Some are in Norfolk breeches, some in short and some in long trousers. Quite a few have jackets too big for them, some too small, with their bony wrists hanging from tight sleeves, but almost all sport Eton collars and stout boots.

The girls, carefully separated from the boys by the width of the lane, wear black stockings and boots, white starched pinafores over their frocks, and some have hats as well. Altogether there must be around seventy children in this photograph. The staff seems to be hidden by the throng, with the exception of one stolid-looking young man who towers above the girls.

I looked in vain for Miss Clare who must have been there at that time, but either she was absent that day or was engulfed by her charges somewhere at the rear of the party.

The school building looked exactly the same, and I recognized several trees as old friends, although considerably shorter. But a magnificent barn, end on to the road, has now gone. The rough grass still grows as thickly at the edge of the lane, and one small child holds a flower to his face, enjoying its scent forever.

With so many memories crowding upon me during this centenary year, I found this scene particularly moving, and shall always be grateful to Mr Lamb for presenting me with such an irreplaceable treasure.

*

With the end of term in sight I conferred with Miss Briggs about our plans. It seemed wise to let parents know in good time about our centenary affairs, especially those who might have costumes to prepare.

'After all, it is *next term*,' I pointed out, 'and Fairacre folk don't like to be hurried into things.'

'I should think that seldom happens,' replied my assistant. 'I've never met such a slow lot of parents. It's about time Fairacre moved with the times, and woke up.'

I was too taken aback by this attack to answer for a moment. Talk about the pot calling the kettle black, was my first reaction!

'And I'm beginning to wonder,' she went on, 'if I don't owe it to myself to change to a livelier job.'

I hardly liked to point out that she had had some months of unemployment before she landed the Fairacre post. Also that she would need a glowing reference from me, which in all honesty I could not supply, to take her to another job, and in any case her probationary year had at least another term to run.

'If you do decide to try your luck,' I said at last, 'you know how much notice you must give. But if you'll take my advice I should get all the experience you can here before you think of changing.'

'Nothing seems to *happen* here!' cried my discontented assistant. 'I should think Fairacre School was exactly like this a hundred years ago! And, as far as I can see, it will be exactly the same a hundred years hence!'

Privately I hoped it would be, but I know full well that the wind of change buffets us daily, and that a school which has shrunk from that thriving community in Mr Lamb's photograph to the twenty-odd children who now comprise the school cannot hope to survive long.

'I think you must make an effort to join some activity or other which you'll enjoy in Caxley,' I said. 'What about the Operatic Society, or Caxley Dramatic Club? You like tennis, I know, and there are two good clubs in Caxley which you might enjoy. At least you would meet other young people. I know it must be pretty lonely for you here with no other young staff.'

'No one's asked me to join anything,' muttered Miss Briggs sulkily.

I began to feel my small stock of patience becoming as exhausted as Herr Hitler's.

'Well of course they haven't! They don't know you are *there*! Go along to a meeting, or find out the name of the secretary, and say you want to join. It's up to you. You can't expect these organizations to search the highways and byways.'

'I don't know if I shall have time, with all this centenary fuss to arrange,' said Miss Briggs, as though the entire burden of our celebrations rested on her dandruff-sprinkled shoulders.

I took a deep breath.

'Which brings us to the point. You'd better come to tea tomorrow and we'll draft out our plan.'

'I wash my hair tomorrow after school,' she said.

Far be it from me to stop that, was my unworthy thought.

'Make it Friday,' I said shortly, and got out the register.

Amy called the following evening, and I was glad that Miss Briggs was elsewhere attending to her hair. I enquired after the progress of the autobiography.

'Well, it's uphill work, I can tell you! As you know, I always think one's childhood is the most interesting part of an autobiography. But then, where does one begin?'

'I should think: "I was born on May the Whatever in Nether Wallop or Somesuch."'

'I feel that's too bald. I think people are glad to be told

something about one's parents, but I dread going back too far and having sixteen, if not thirty-two, dubious portraits of forebears on each side.'

'I rather agree.'

'On the other hand, there were some very colourful ancestors on my mother's side. Two brothers were transported to Australia for stealing sheep and cattle.' Amy spoke with considerable pride.

'Well, put 'em in,' I advised.

'It would certainly swell the volume a little. You've no idea how much writing is needed to make a page of print. It's really quite daunting. I'm thinking of throwing in a distant great-uncle too. He was defrocked sometime in the last century for conduct not befitting the clergy. Something to do with the choir boys, I gather, but it's so difficult to find any clear evidence after all this time.'

'I'd no idea you had such a disreputable background, Amy.'

'My immediate background is blameless,' she assured me. 'And very dull too. My grandparents and parents seem to have worked hard, kept out of debt, looked after their small families, and generally been worthy and respectable. The consequence is that they make pretty dull reading matter, and I wonder if it might be a good idea to start farther back. I could have a family tree in the front.'

'Does anyone ever look at them? All I find is that having pulled the thing out, it is impossible to fold it correctly again, and you have a yard of tissue paper in your lap all the time you are reading.'

'That's true,' agreed Amy. 'But going back to your first idea of plunging straight in with one's birth – do you think readers are *really gripped* by hearing about your being bottle fed and having your adenoids out, and the way you had hysterics at the age of four when Father Christmas kissed you, reeking of whisky?'

'All those things might create a sympathetic bond,' I said. 'As these confounded educationists tell us *ad nauseam*, children should be able to identify themselves with the characters they are reading about. Though how you can identify with Sinbad the Sailor or Tom Thumb beats me.'

'Well, all I can say is that I have spent a good hour after tea every day for the past fortnight, pushing along my reluctant ball point, and I don't suppose I have written enough to fill four pages of a real book. It's very disheartening.'

'Cheer up!' I said. 'Think how splendid it will look piled up in the book shops with queues outside fighting to get in to buy it. And you on television. Possibly on *This Is Your Life*. Just think of that!'

'I refuse to consider it,' said Amy firmly.

Mrs Partridge, the vicar's wife, called at the school the next morning, and the children sat up with smiles wreathing their faces.

They like Mrs Partridge. I like to think it is for herself alone, for she is a kind, warm-hearted person and devoted to the young, but I have the feeling that she is welcomed more for the bag of boiled sweets which she so often brings with her.

Today was no exception, except that the sweets were toffees and not fruit drops. The children's response to this largesse was ecstatic, as Patrick handed round the bag.

'Now, my dear,' said Mrs Partridge when all were busy sucking. 'I wonder if you can do me a favour.'

What answer is there to that after such generosity?

'Of course,' I said rashly.

'I'm short of collectors for my *Save The Children* flag day next week, and I wondered if you could help.'

'Where would you want me to go?' I asked, resigned to my lot.

'Well, I'm doing from The Beetle and Wedge to the crossroads, and Margaret Waters is doing the other side of the road, and Joan Benson was to have done that outlying part from her house to Tyler's Row, but she has had to hare off to look at a couple of houses her daughter has found. It is that stretch that I hoped you might find time to do.'

I agreed to take over Joan's territory, and Mrs Partridge whipped a piece of paper from the top of the basket she was carrying, and placed a collecting tin on my desk with incredible speed.

'That's *most* kind of you, dear,' she said briskly. 'Could you let me have it back by Thursday? And here is your official badge, and the flags.'

The piece of paper had successfully hidden all these things in the basket, and I noticed yet another collecting tin and more flags, still to be allotted presumably.

'I'll do that,' I promised. Bang go the two evenings I had earmarked for making strawberry jam and bottling cherries, I thought!

She wished the children good-bye, and they replied with their diction somewhat impeded by toffee, but true love shining in their eyes.

The door had hardly closed before Eileen Burton was sick on the floor, and one of the Coggs twins began to choke on a large piece of sweet which had gone down the wrong way.

I hastily put the collecting box on the window sill before going to the rescue.

Save The Children indeed! What about the teachers?

Miss Briggs duly stayed late on Friday, and accompanied me to the school house for tea. She appeared somewhat monosyllabic and sulky, but whether she was feeling resentful at staying after school, or whether she was simply being natural – Mr Willet's 'a fair old lump of a girl' came to mind – I could not say.

However, she cheered up a little after three cups of tea, brown bread and honey followed by a large slice of Dundee cake, and we settled down with pencils and notebooks to our task.

'I think six scenes will be ample,' I said, 'which means something from the reigns of Victoria, Edward the Seventh, George the Fifth, Edward the Eighth – unless we leave him out – George the Sixth, and our present Queen.'

'Good idea,' agreed Miss Briggs, sucking a sticky finger. 'If we had a scene for every decade that would make . . . how many?'

'Ten,' I told her. 'You ought to know that – child of the metric system as you are.'

'Yes, well – if we had the scenes lasting only ten minutes that would be far too long, wouldn't it?'

'My feeling entirely. We can't expect people to sit on the school seats for more than an hour altogether, and if we have a few songs, and then tea afterwards it is as much as the human frame can take.'

'Have you found some likely stories from the log book?'

'One or two. I thought for the first scene we could use the boy Pratt putting on the school clock, and being caught by the headmistress.'

'Lovely! But how will he climb up? Would he pile up the desks?'

I repressed a shudder.

'No. We'll have Mr Willet's step ladder to hand. After all, it just *may* have been left in the schoolroom. And through all the scenes we'll use the old side desk, and the actors will be in period costume, of course. When we get to Elizabeth the Second we can push on a modern desk. The old style were in use when I first came here. I must say, they were pretty sturdy.'

'Then what?' asked my assistant, bringing me back to the work in hand.

'Well, for Edward the Seventh, I thought it would be marvellous if I could say something like: "It was in this reign that a new pupil teacher took up her duties", and in walks Miss Clare!'

'Perfect!'

'Then she could tell us about her experiences of that time. I have sounded her, and she's game to do it. Frankly, I think it will be the high spot of the whole proceedings.'

'What about George the Fifth?'

'I think it will have to have something to do with the Great War.'

I told her about Miss Clare's memories of the babies fraying pieces of cotton material to make field dressings. We could enlarge on the helping-the-war-effort theme, without dwelling unduly on the horrors which many of the older people in the audience would remember all too well. I wondered if one of the parents who went as a child from Fairacre School to the Wembley Exhibition might give an enthusiastic first-hand account of a country child's memories of that memorable charabanc ride to London in the twenties. Mr Lamb perhaps? Or Mrs Willet? I promised to follow up the idea.

The more we thought about Edward the Eighth's brief reign the stronger became our resolve to leave out a scene, and simply let the narrator comment on that passage of time. Apart from the Abdication, which really had very little impact on the children of the school, there was little to mark the reign's fleeting impression on the village.

The 1939–45 war, which followed within three years, had much more effect, of course, and we resolved to show the crowded desks, with the gas mask boxes lodged thereupon, and one or two wartime posters pinned up – as evidently there had been in Mr Fortescue's session as headmaster at that time. Luckily, Mr Willet still had two precious relics, one showing the results of careless talk and the other of wasting food. There were one or two incidents in the log book which could form the basis of a scene, and perhaps Mrs Austen of Springbourne might be prevailed upon to give her impression of Fairacre School from an evacuee's point of view.

As for our last, and present-day, scene, what could be better than drawing the audience's attention to the children's exhibition of work in both rooms, singing by the whole school, and the narrator pointing out such facts as the vanishing of those over eleven to the local comprehensive school and cutting down the numbers of Fairacre School drastically after the 1944 Act?

Finally, I had asked the vicar if he would appear at the end and remind us all that the church had always played an important part in the hundred years of Fairacre School. He was willing to do this, and to end our proceedings with a prayer for blessings received in the past, and our hopes for the future.

'That should take us up to tea very nicely,' said Miss Briggs kindly.

'We'll all need it by then,' I assured her. 'And now let's rough out which children would be best as the actors.'

It took us until nearly seven o'clock, but we felt it had been worth it. Certainly, Miss Briggs departed looking very much more cheerful than when she arrived, and had been surprisingly helpful.

The weather had been perfect, at least in my eyes, for the last few weeks of term. The sun had shone from a cloudless sky, every playtime had found the schoolroom deserted and the playground crowded with good-tempered children playing with unusual placidity. But I was surprised, nevertheless, to hear that an official drought had been declared, and we were all being exhorted to save water.

It always beats me how, in the temperate climate we are supposed to enjoy, panic sets in as soon as any mild and foreseen variations from the normal weather conditions prevail. If three inches of snow fall in January, the head-lines scream about disrupted rail services, motorway chaos, children marooned in school buses and lambs dying in drifts. The country, they say dramatically, has been brought to a standstill. They seem to cope pretty well in Canada, or America and Switzerland, it seems to me, with about thirty times the amount of precipitation.

And why, as in the present circumstances, have we to watch each precious drop of water? Way back in February, we were sloshing about knee-deep in the stuff, as the swollen rivers overflowed, and Mr Roberts was out rescuing lambs at Springbourne.

In any event, we were all blissfully happy in the scorch-ing sun, and I scuffed through the dust at the edge of the road on my way to the grocer's after school, glorying in the heat. It was beginning to look like the end of summer, with the grass drying prematurely and even some yellow leaves appearing on the fruit trees. Miss Waters's privet hedge was in flower, the small white pyramids of blossom giving out that faint sickly smell which is the essence of summer.

White convolvulus plants scrambled along the wire fence which borders the post office garden, the purity of their trumpets sadly tarnished with dust and heat. Below them, a root of scarlet poppies flamed, giving out their hot peppery fragrance as the dry wind shook them.

I met the vicar as I returned. He greeted me cheerfully and told me that his bees were extremely active.

'No more swarms?'

'Not yet, but this is the sort of weather that might set them off,' he told me. 'The swarm I collected from Margaret Waters has settled in beautifully. Very attractive bees – rather paler than my first, and so busy! Really they are an example to one in this heat. I must confess I find it most trying, and shall welcome the rain when it comes.'

Mr Willet hailed me from the churchyard when I was nearly home, and I walked across to see him. It was cool in the shade of the massive yew tree where I stood. Mr Willet was busy cutting long grass from some of the ancient burial mounds with a bill-hook.

'Hot work,' I commented.

'Suits me,' said my caretaker, mopping his glistening face. He came and stood beside me, and together we surveyed the sleeping place of the Fairacre dead. It was all very peaceful. Some midges drifted in clouds near the hedge, and a peacock butterfly opened and shut its beautiful wings upon the warm stone slab commemorating some village worthy.

With the centenary always to the front of my mind these days, I wondered how many of those resting here had attended the little school hard by, and what they had thought of it. As if reading my thoughts, Mr Willet said that there was a mort of folk these days as preferred to go up in smoke, and he wondered if it was right.

'We certainly miss all those lovely inscriptions,' I said. 'Personally, I enjoy a potter round this churchyard reading about virtuous wives and devoted mothers mourned by their fourteen sorrowing children. I've even got a soft spot for that terrible marble angel in memory of Mr Parr who died in 1870, "Benefactor and Brother To All".'

'Nice bit of work,' agreed Mr Willet. 'I likes a bit of white marble myself. Can't take to that polished pink granite. Might just as well have a bit of cold brawn on top of you, from the looks of it.'

'Well, I must go home,' I said reluctantly. 'Tibby expects a meal.'

'You spoils that cat. It'll get fatty heart the way you feeds it.'

'She's got a large frame,' I protested.

'Not surprising, the amount she packs away,' replied Mr Willet. 'I'd better get on too. There's plenty of old Fairacre pupils wants tidying up by the south wall. You ever thought of that? You'll maybe get some ghosts at them celebrations of yours.'

'I rather hope we shall,' I said, stepping round the gravestone of one Sally Gray who died in 1890 in her 63rd year. She would have been fifty-three when Fairacre School was newly built, I thought, making my way home through the heat.

How the history of this little village pressed around one!

Obedient to Mrs Partridge's behest, I set off on my collecting stint one hot evening.

For once, clouds covered the sky. They were ominously dark, but made no appreciable difference to the heat. It was about to break, and I only hoped that I should get my job done before that happened.

People were generous with their donations, and my tin was soon quite heavy, and chiefly with silver, not copper coins. I had left Joan Benson's house until last, as it was the furthest from home, and I could then have an uninterrupted walk back to feed my overweight cat at the right time.

A few drops of rain began to patter against the holly hedge round the garden as I opened the gate. All the windows were shut, including those in Miriam Quinn's annexe at the side, and there was that indefinable feeling of blankness that always seems to emanate from a deserted house. However, I decided to try my luck. I remembered that Joan had been going to look at a house near her daughter's, but hoped that she would have returned.

I was unlucky. No one answered the bell, and the rain began to fall in torrents. I was well sheltered in the deep porch, and sat down on a sturdy bench which ran along one side to watch the downpour.

It was wonderful to see the plants reviving in the heavy shower. The dusty drive was soon pock-marked with large raindrops, and then with tiny rivulets that snaked their way downhill to the gate. The holly hedge began to glisten with drops, and the thirsty flowers in the parched border seemed to lift their heads in response to this benison of refreshing rain.

Drops began to stream from the porch, until I began to feel that I was surveying the garden through a curtain of glass beads. The smell of water on hot stone rose all around me, and I began to realize how desperately the earth had been waiting for the rain.

It was obvious that Miriam Quinn had not returned yet from the office in Caxley. It was quite likely that there would be flooding there, I surmised, for the river Cax overflows very readily, and the low-lying parts of the town, particularly the area known as 'The Marsh' floods with depressing regularity, despite the efforts of drainage experts to control this nuisance.

But my spirits rose when I heard a car scrunching up the back drive on the wet gravel. Here, no doubt, was Miriam returning. But I was wrong. The car did not stop at the annexe, but swept up to the porch where I was sitting, and pulled up with a squealing of brakes.

Out of the car leapt Henry Mawne, head down through the blinding rain, and met me face to face.

'Good Lord! Have you rung?'

'Yes, but there's no one at home. I was waiting for the worst of the rain to go.'

Henry looked agitated. He jingled some coins in his pocket, and bounced up and down on his toes, gazing at the watery scene.

'Oh dear! Oh dear! Now I wonder when she will be back. Any idea?'

'None at all, I'm afraid.'

I told him about Joan's departure for her house hunting.

'Well, let me give you a lift back. You might be stuck here for hours. It looks as though it has set in for the night.'

I was very grateful, and we drove back through the glistening lanes, with the rain drumming on the roof of the car, and the windscreen wipers working away like maniacs.

'Come in,' I said, when we drew up at my front door, but he refused.

'It's about Joan's house,' he began, rather explosively. 'Is it still on the market, do you know?'

I said I thought it was.

'We've been in Ireland for the past three weeks, looking up relatives there, and I missed *The Caxley Chronicle*'s advertisement. You see, I was wondering if it would suit David and Irene.'

'Do they know about it?'

'No, that's the point. I thought Joan might let me have a look, and if I thought it a possibility I would tell them on the telephone, and they could come down at once to view. It seems to me that you have to work at the speed of light these days, if you want to buy a house. What's she asking for it?'

Again I had to confess ignorance. I really wanted to get into my own abode, but Henry seemed to want to unburden himself.

'I do wish you'd come in,' I urged him, but he was adamant. He sat staring straight ahead through the rain-beaded windscreen, his fingers drumming on the wheel, and a little nerve twitching in his cheek.

'It's all very difficult. I know they hope to move from the London house, and get further out. Better for Simon too, in the holidays. Better for all of them when you think of what David and the boy went through there when poor Teresa lost her sanity.'

I murmured sympathetically. I knew only too well how strung up that young boy had been when he had been one of my pupils for a few summer weeks.

'On the other hand, I don't want to interfere. A second marriage can always be a bit dicey, I think, and they may loathe the idea of being near us, or any relatives, for that matter. But this place looks about the right size for them. Three bedrooms, I believe?'

'And the annexe,' I said.

'But surely Miriam Quinn's in that?'

'She is at the moment.'

'Nice woman. I shouldn't think Irene and David would want her to go.'

There was silence for a time. The rain continued to throb relentlessly above and around us. A few blackbirds scrabbled joyfully under the bushes, enjoying the softened soil after the hard surface of the past weeks.

'He has regular trips these days to Holland, Belgium and Norway, so Irene would be glad of Miriam next door, I should imagine. And it's only an hour's drive to Heathrow. It took him pretty well that time to get across London.'

I could see that he was thinking aloud, putting the pros and cons to himself, and really attempting to make a decision.

'I should simply ring David and let him think it over,' I said, stating the obvious.

To my surprise, he seized my hands in his and shook them warmly. 'An excellent notion!' he exclaimed. 'After all, it's his decision, isn't it?'

He leant across to open the door for me, beaming the while.

'Yes, I'll do that immediately. What a help you've been!'

He sped off, cutting short my thanks, and I entered to be greeted by my starving Tibby.

While she wolfed down raw liver I sipped a drink and thought, for the umpteenth time, about this business of buying a house.

For years I have meant to do it. After all, the time flies by, and when I reached retirement age I should have to have somewhere to live. Now that Fairacre School's numbers had sunk perilously low, I might well find myself homeless if the school were closed.

I felt reasonably sure that I would not be turned out into the snow like some Victorian heroine. I might even be offered the house first, if it were to be sold, as no doubt it would be eventually. In any case, I should get plenty of notice to quit, if it came to that. But the thing was, where should I go? Somewhere nearby would be ideal.

And secondly, what should I use for money? My meagre savings might rise to a deposit on the house, but would a building society give me a mortgage at my age?

I had been a fool not to buy when prices were less astronomic, as Amy pointed out when she called one afternoon.

'I've told you time and time again,' she said severely. 'And you've done nothing all these years.'

'I know,' I said meekly. 'Well, I've just lived from day to day. And jolly nice it's been,' I added defiantly.

Amy laughed. 'Well, my dear old silly, you know you can always have a bed at Bent, if the worse comes to the worst.' She looked at me speculatively. 'How much could you raise if you saw something you liked?'

I told her.

'It would hardly buy the bathroom,' she said. 'Would you let me lend you some money?'

'No, indeed!' I said.

'I've got quite a nice little nest egg, and you might just as well have some of it. Think it over, anyway.'

'You are sweet to think of it, but honestly I couldn't possibly accept.'

'Well, the offer will stand, darling,' said Amy, getting up to go.

'Besides, if I bought now, I should have to let it while I'm still teaching, and you know how impossible it is to get tenants out if they dig in their heels. No, I think I must just soldier on as I am. Lord knows I'm happy enough this way.'

'Bless you, so you are! And as the old song says: "You die if you worry, You die if you don't, So why worry at all?"'

And on this cheering note Amy departed.

'Nice drop of rain,' commented Mrs Pringle, with unwonted affability the next morning. 'My lettuces have picked up wonderful, and the water butt's full again.'

I said it seemed to have done a lot of good everywhere except for the aperture where the skylight once had pride of place. A fine puddle had cascaded on to the tarpaulin and thence to the floor. Luckily, I had been prudent enough to shift my desk during these protracted building operations, or we should have had more serious damage.

Mrs Pringle's countenance assumed its usual gloom as she surveyed the mess. 'I'll have a straight word with Reg Thorn when I see him,' she boomed.

I felt a pang of sympathy for the poor wretch, maddening though he was. He would meet his match in Mrs Pringle.

The delays and confusion which had accompanied the

removal of the skylight and the replacement by a simple dormer window had to be seen to be believed. It seemed to me that Reg Thorn was constantly driving to the builder's merchant, or the timber yard, in Caxley, to acquire or replace new pieces of window equipment which surely should have been bought at the beginning and assembled in his own workshop. What he spent in petrol alone must have made a hole in the taxpayers' pockets, but I suppose none of his fuming customers could get at him whilst in transit, so that from his point of view he was leading a comparatively peaceful life.

Mrs Pringle began to mop up, muttering to herself the while and clanging the bucket. I looked up a hymn for morning prayers before getting Ernest to ring the school bell to alert any stragglers still in the lanes or fields of Fairacre.

These last few days of term are always busy. This time, the last week seemed fuller than ever, for I wanted to visit the parents of the principal actors to see their reaction to making costumes for the favoured few.

Linda Moffat was to be one of the stars as Miss Richards, the first headmistress of Fairacre School. It was she who caned John Pratt in July 1882, and we had cast Patrick, who is small but with a good loud voice, as the youthful sinner. Mrs Moffat is a skilful dressmaker, and I felt sure that she would not only make Linda's costume superbly, but would be generous enough to lend a hand with the others if need be.

I also rang Mrs Austen to sound her out about her contribution of an evacuee's memories to our performance. To my joy, she was most enthusiastic and promised to prepare a script which we could discuss.

Altogether it was a satisfactory ending to the school year. There was a chance of another family coming to live in the village, as Mr Roberts had engaged a new shepherd who had three children. This was encouraging as it would mean an increase next term in my dangerously low numbers. The sun appeared again after the storm and, apart from the annoyance of the skylight non-activity, all appeared hopeful in my little world.

The vicar called to wish the children a happy holiday, and added his usual rider about helping their mothers. This was followed by the ritual: 'The same to you, sir!' which is always considered the height of humour by my pupils.

They dispersed boisterously into the summer sunshine, and as their voices died away down the lane, I wandered across to the school house, rejoicing in the long weeks of blissful freedom ahead.

8. August

My holiday plans were simple. The first few days had been spent in coping with neglected jobs such as weeding the border and washing the kitchen paintwork.

I had made arrangements to spent a fortnight in Norfolk with an old friend, and meanwhile Miss Clare had accepted an invitation from me to spend a few days at Fairacre at the beginning of the month.

The spare room lay in an unusual state of pristine splendour. The furniture gleamed from Mrs Pringle's ministrations. The feather bed was beautifully puffed up beneath a fresh chintz bedspread. On the table at the bedside was a posy of all the sweetest-smelling flowers I had been able to pick in the garden. Lavender, roses, pinks and a sprig or two of night-scented stock made a handsome nosegay in a little lustre jug which had once been my mother's.

I had been invited to tea at Miss Clare's, and went over to fetch her with a buoyant heart. I always enjoy visiting that neat cottage, thatched by Dolly Clare's father when the family first went to live there. It had two downstairs rooms, both of good size, and two bedrooms above. A little bathroom had been added when main water had come, at long last, to Beech Green some years ago.

The garden was large for a cottage. Miss Clare still kept the front one tidy and gay with flowers, but the larger part at the back was used as a vegetable plot by a young man in the village who was glad to have the produce for his large family. He kept Dolly supplied with all that she needed, so that it was an ideal arrangement.

The best white cloth had been spread in my honour, and the thin ancient teaspoons of silver gleamed brightly. The best tea set, with a pretty pattern of pansies, was in evidence, and the usual plate of wafer-thin bread and butter and a splendid sponge cake, which I knew would be as light as a feather, showed that the mistress of the house had been busy.

Beyond the lattice windowpane the downs shimmered in a blue heat haze. It was a tranquil spot and Dolly Clare had lived there from the age of six, first with her family, and then alone for a number of years. To her great joy, her lifelong friend Emily Davis had joined her for several years, and the two old ladies had lived in perfect harmony until Emily's death a few years earlier.

Much had happened under this old thatched roof. The joys and griefs of a family, the sharing of a nation's wars, and always the relentless pressure of poverty. But it was a happy house; one felt it as soon as one crossed the threshold. Here was a haven, a quiet backwater where one could rest tranquilly away from the turbulent mainstream of life. This blessed peace, I well knew, stemmed mainly from the quiet spirit who lived there, but even without her presence one was conscious of a home which had been loved by many generations.

'I have been given some nerine bulbs,' said Miss Clare, entering with the tea pot. 'Do you know anything about them?'

'They say that if they like you they grow like weeds. If not, you'll never be able to rear them.'

'We'll live in hope then. George Annett says they need lots of manure, but Bob Willet says the exact opposite! Lots of sandy soil at the foot of a south-facing wall, was his advice.'

'Why not do that, and bung on lots of manure in the autumn? That way you are hedging your bets, I should think.'

'I remember seeing them years ago in Devon, when a

friend took me away for a few days at the October half-term. So many of the gardens had great clumps of these beautiful rose-pink heads. I've never felt I could afford to buy them, but now I've been given some I should grieve if I mistreated them.'

I promised that we would look up the care of nerines in my new gardening book the minute we were home, and our conversation turned to her contribution to the centenary celebrations.

'I am quite looking forward to it,' said Dolly, carefully folding a thin slice of bread and butter. 'I suppose I ought to feel nervous, but I'm not, you know. After all, most of those present will be old pupils of mine. And that particular period, in King Edward's time, was a very happy one for me. I was a pupil teacher for several years then at Fairacre School, and dear Emily was my constant companion. We were so lucky to have Mr Wardle as our headmaster. He was a cheerful soul, and always out to help us both.'

'And you and Emily stayed together?'

'Well, no. She found a post south of Caxley, and I can't tell you how I missed her. We met when we could and caught up with our news, and exchanged our views on teaching. And if we met in Caxley, we went window shopping. That's all we could afford.'

Miss Clare laughed. 'We were very short of money. Everybody was. I don't suppose there was a single child at Fairacre School in those days who wasn't dressed in secondhand clothes. They were handed down from one child to the next, and gratefully received from any of the more well-to-do families. As for jumble sales, they were serious shopping expeditions then, not just an afternoon's spree in the village. I had a tweed cape cut down from a full-sized one of poor Miss Lilian's, which I wore for years.'

Poor Miss Lilian, I remembered, had been the feeble-minded daughter of one of the leading families in Beech Green. It was a never-to-be-forgotten tragedy that she and her mother perished on the *Titanic* in 1912 as they crossed the Atlantic to consult an eminent American brain surgeon in the hope of effecting Lilian's recovery.

'I think shortage of money was the chief worry then. There wasn't so much concern with health. As long as you could keep going and earn a bit, you tended to ignore minor aches and pains, and perhaps it was a good thing, although people often struggled on when really they should have gone to the doctor. But he needed paying, you see. It was all an uphill struggle, and I know many of the children came hungry to school. The older people could remember the rebellion of some of the agricultural workers when they smashed machinery, and shouted for bread. When I see the bonny children of today, and remember some of those in my early classes, I feel thankful that times have changed.'

'You'll talk about this, I hope, when you give us your memories?'

'Indeed I will,' said Miss Clare with spirit, 'for now I think too much is taken for granted, and thankfulness is becoming as dead as perseverance and truthfulness and a great many other fine old-fashioned virtues.'

She sat back from the table and looked through the window at the tall hollyhocks outside. From her pensive expression I knew that her thoughts were years away.

She took a deep breath, and gave me her sweet smile.

'Well, shall we be going?'

We cleared away, and Dolly went slowly round the house, closing windows and locking doors.

Within half an hour we were travelling along the familiar lane which Dolly had traversed daily for many years, in fair weather and foul, until St Patrick's church spire pierced the skyline, and we were back in Fairacre again and looking up 'Nerines' in my latest gardening book.

Mr Willet turned up the next morning, balancing a pair of shears on the bars of his bicycle.

'Promised I'd do that box edging,' he shouted through the kitchen window. 'All right to tackle it now? Got a wedding this afternoon.'

'Hello, Bob,' said Miss Clare, appearing in the doorway.

'Well, I'm blowed!' said Mr Willet beaming. 'And how be you keeping, Dolly? You looks younger than ever. Got some magic secret, have you?'

Dolly Clare laughed. 'I don't say much about my aches and pains, Bob. Doesn't do any good, and bores people stiff.'

'I tells everyone if I've got a finger ache,' replied Mr Willet robustly. 'Makes me feel a durn sight better when I've unloaded all my woes on to someone else.'

She followed her old friend into the sunshine, and I watched them talking animatedly as Bob Willet surveyed the job to be tackled. They would have plenty of gossip to exchange, I guessed.

Reg Thorn's business was closed for a fortnight's holiday, so that we were spared the racket of banging tools, the boys' transistor and their vigorous exchange of opinions over football and cricket matters.

When I carried out the coffee cups some time later, the sun was so hot that we dragged my ancient deckchairs into the shade of the apple tree.

'Funny how you can drink hot coffee winter and summer,' commented Mr Willet, drying his moustache on the back of his hand, 'and still it do you a power of good.'

'They're a fine pair of shears,' observed Dolly, eyeing the shining blades resting on the grass by Bob's feet.

'Yes, well, I likes my own tools. Miss Read here do have a pair of shears – so-called – but they does more harm than good, twizzling up the sappy bits and wrenching away at the twiggy bits like a host of rats 'ad been at work.'

'Thanks,' I said.

'No need to be sarky,' said Mr Willet amiably. 'Some knows how to look after tools, and some don't, that's all I'm saying.'

He struggled from the deck chair.

'I suppose I'd best get on. You women would keep me here all morning with your gossiping.'

'Well – !' I began.

'By the way, I see that young Simon in the village as I come up here. He staying with the Mawnes d'you know?'

'I hadn't heard. How does he look?'

'Much the same as ever – a long streak of nothin', and lookin' as though butter wouldn't melt in his mouth, the young varmint. When I think of our Snowy as he did in, I could give that boy a leathering and enjoy it!'

Mr Willet's face grew puce at the remembrance of Simon's part in the death of Fairacre's albino robin not so long ago. I decided to change the subject.

'Any chance of seeing you here tomorrow?'

'Ah! I might manage that if I'm spared. This edging of yours will need a few hours on it, the state it's got into.'

I picked up the tray, and left Dolly to watch her old friend at work.

In the kitchen, putting the cups to soak, I wondered if Simon's parents had come to Fairacre to have a look at Joan Benson's house. I did not propose to mention this possibility to anyone, as I did not want to spread any rumours. However, no matter how prudently I held my tongue, there was no doubt in my mind that whatever was decided under the Mawnes' or the Bensons' roofs would very soon be common knowledge in our little community.

Miss Clare was with me for a week, and the weather stayed sunny for all that time. We took picnic lunches up on the downs, or down by the little brook at Springbourne, as it purled along beneath drooping willows on its way to join the Cax before the river flowed through Caxley. Everywhere we went held memories for Dolly and, like all old people, her early years were clearer in her mind than more recent ones.

I found her recollections fascinating, and only wished I had a recording machine with me all the time. It certainly made me decide to get one ready for the centenary day when I could record her talk for future generations. Dolly's lifetime spanned the age-old rural life of hard work geared to the pace of man and horse, and modern life geared to the pace of cars, lorries and aircraft. Children of Dolly's generation were lucky to have travelled twenty miles from home. Many of them had never seen the sea, some sixty or seventy miles distant, nor travelled in a train, nor visited a town any larger than Caxley.

Their grandchildren thought nothing of flying anywhere across the globe, of talking to relatives in New Zealand as they sat by their own firesides, and of buying the produce of the world set out temptingly at the village shop. Once Dolly and her contemporaries had gone, the way of life which had been known and expressed in poetry, prose and pictures for centuries would vanish. It was a sobering thought.

But it was the small personal memories that I cherished as we took our drives around the countryside which Dolly knew so well.

'That was where old Mrs Johns lived,' she said as we passed a tumbledown cottage with a collapsed roof of

thatch. 'She wore a bustle, you know, till the end of her life. A funny little soul, who kept that place spotless.'

'Ernie White was killed in that field,' she commented. 'A tractor tipped over and pinned the poor soul there for hours. People said it was a judgement for doing away with the horses.'

She sighed.

'And that's where Emily's Edgar lived. She should have been there by rights, but he married his nurse, you know, and my dear Emily never got over it, brave face though she showed to the world.'

She showed me where she and Emily tobogganned as children, where she took her pupils to collect hazel nuts and frogspawn, and then holly to decorate St Patrick's church at Christmas time. It was borne in upon me how closely the seasons were woven into the fabric of the country child's life in those days. They were out so much more than today's children. They walked everywhere. No school buses whisked them past beds of violets, wild strawberries, sprays of luscious blackberries, all known and treasured by their grandparents.

One afternoon, I invited Mrs Austen to tea and it was a rare treat for me to listen to the war-time reminiscences of evacuee and teacher at Fairacre School in the early forties.

'Everything was so different from our home and school at New Cross in south London,' said Mrs Austen. 'For one thing, I was used to an enormous three-storey building with infants on the ground floor, big girls on the next, and boys at the top. It was lovely to be mixed up together, such a *few* of us it seemed, in a dear little school like Fairacre's.'

'You certainly settled down wonderfully,' commented Miss Clare.

'I think I found the biggest differences, though, at Mrs

Pratt's, where we were billeted. She couldn't have been kinder, and I kept in touch with her until she died, but there were some things which shook me as a child. No flush lavatory for one. And lighting lamps and candles, instead of switching on the electric light. I dreaded having to go down the garden to the privy in the dark. Mrs Pratt used to light a hurricane lamp for me, but it cast such shadows I was even more terrified.'

'Was there no commode in your bedroom?' enquired Miss Clare with concern.

'Well, yes – but I hated using it. It seemed so *wrong* to me. I'd never met such a thing, you see. And another thing that appalled me was the number of flies everywhere, and all taken for granted. At home, in London, my mother bustled a stray fly away as if it were poisonous – which it was, I always thought – but Mrs Pratt even had a paper ball hung up near the ceiling and called it the flies' playground.'

'We had one too, I remember,' said Miss Clare.

'There was another ball on the mantelpiece made of silver paper. We all collected every scrap of tin foil and it was carefully wrapped round the ball. It was an enormous weight. I can't think what happened to it eventually.'

'It went to the hospital in Caxley,' Miss Clare told her. 'Still does, I believe, but now they like it flat.'

'I was very fond of Mrs Pratt,' said Mrs Austen, 'but frightened of her old mother who lived down the road. Do you remember that little boy – I forget his name – who lived with her?'

'I do indeed,' said Dolly. 'He was called Stephen, a foster-child, and really old Mrs Hall had no business to have him. She was far too frail and suffered from tuberculosis, and in any case much too ancient to take care of a young child. But it was difficult to find homes for those orphans, and I suppose the local authority thought it was suitable. In any case, the Halls needed the maintenance money, but I was glad when that child was moved else-where.'

'So was I! I used to collect him to bring him along to school, and the smell in that house was ghastly. And the poor old thing was always coughing. She used to crouch on the rag rug in front of the fire with the ash pan pulled out, and spit horribly into the hot ashes. Sometimes she had no breath to speak to me, but just gazed at me with those watery blue eyes and motioned me to take Stephen out of the way. I did too, as quickly as I could.'

'He went into the army eventually,' Dolly told her, 'and did very well. I still hear from him at Christmas, dear boy.'

Her voice was warm with affection. Were there any of her pupils, I wondered, who failed to kindle a spark of remembered happiness in their old teacher? Even the malefactors, dealt with sternly in their youth, were now seen through the rosy haze of time. And why not?

I took Dolly back to her cottage with the greatest reluc-tance, I had enjoyed her serene company so much. But she insisted that she had a number of little household jobs to do, and some bottles of fruit to prepare for the store cupboard, so that I left her looking happy in her shining kitchen with the cat for company.

I went on to Bent to lunch with Amy. I found her house as welcoming and beautiful as Dolly Clare's, although three times the size, of course.

'How do you manage to keep it so immaculate?' I cried. 'I've never seen a speck of dust or one dead flower in this place, all the years I've visited here.'

'Elementary organization,' said Amy. 'You too could have an immaculate house if you planned your routine.'

'You remind me of those advertisements, Amy. "You too can have a beautiful bust".'

'I liked the one about piano-playing in our youth. "You too can be a concert pianist", or something like that.'

'Better than that! "My friends used to laugh when I sat down at the piano." Remember?'

'Mine still do,' said Amy. 'It must be lovely to have a talent of some sort.'

'How's the autobiography?'

'Oh dear, oh dear! I was afraid you'd ask! I'm stuck at myself aged eight, and all I can remember are idiotic things like tying reef knots as a Brownie, and my father cranking up our first family car, and having to help him fix canvas and mica side curtains to it when it rained. I don't think it's very stirring stuff, not a bit like some of these successful memoirs where the authors remember all sorts of psychological hook-ups and traumatic experiences when they found the cat having kittens in the laundry basket. I wonder why they can do it, and I can't?'

'Probably because you have a much more normal mind,' I assured her. 'And anyway, who's to know they didn't make it all up?'

'I never thought of that!'

'Frankly, I should shelve it for a week or two, and go back to it when you feel like it. Anyway, the weather's too good to stick about indoors pushing the pen.'

'I believe you're right. I've hardly been into Caxley at all since starting the book. Incidentally, I saw your young teacher there the last time I was shopping.'

'Our Miss Briggs? I wonder what she was doing in Caxley? I thought she was at home, in one of those spas – Droitwich or Buxton or somewhere up north. Malvern perhaps.'

'Malvern's *west*, dear. She was with a young man, and they appeared to be very affectionate.'

'Well, I'm blowed! Perhaps she came back to collect something, and brought her young man with her from

Harrogate or whatever. It was during the holidays, I take it, that you saw her?'

'Yes, the beginning of last week.'

'Well, I'm glad to hear she's found an interest at last. It may liven her up. Mr Willet calls her "a fair old lump of a girl", and I don't think one can better that description.'

'Poor thing!' said Amy. 'Anyway, she looked quite animated and pretty in the High Street.'

'Ah! The transformation wrought by love! I must try it some time.'

'I wish you would,' said Amy forcefully, returning to a well-worn theme, 'but aren't you leaving it rather late?'

Trust old friends to tell you the unpalatable truth!

Mrs Pringle arrived 'to bottom' me as she elegantly terms performing the house cleaning. Sometimes she only has time 'to put me to rights', and that is bad enough. 'To be bottomed' involves taking down curtains and pictures, pulling out a heavy Welsh dresser and generally creating mayhem. I try and make myself scarce when threatened with bottoming, but on this occasion there was no escape as I was expecting the lawnmower to be returned from the repairer's and wanted to pay him.

Halfway through the dire proceedings I was allowed to pick my way through displaced furniture piled in the kitchen to put on the kettle for a restorative cup of tea.

Mrs Pringle, militant in a flowered overall with the sleeves rolled up to expose wrestler's forearms, had a fanatical look in her eyes.

'You seen the top of that dresser of yours?' she asked.

'No. What's wrong with it?'

'*Wrong with it?*' echoed Mrs Pringle triumphantly. 'It's got two inches of dust on it as you could grow potatoes in.'

'Oh, come . . .' I began weakly.

'And what's more, down the back, was a letter unopened and dated months ago.'

'Good heavens! Where is it?'

Mrs Pringle handed me an envelope. The address was handwritten, and I recognized it as Lucy Clayton's writing. She had been at college with Amy and me, and I cordially detested her.

'No one that matters,' I said with some relief, and made the tea.

We took it into the garden. The sight of my house I found upsetting.

'Well, I must say it's a treat to breathe a bit of clean air after all that dust and filth,' announced Mrs Pringle, stirring her tea. 'You heard about Mrs Partridge?'

'No. What's happened?'

'She had to go to hospital, poor soul.'

I was genuinely shocked. I am devoted to our vicar's wife, and the thought of her in hospital was even more upsetting than the chaos in my house.

'When did she go?'

'Last Saturday.'

'And it's Wednesday today! I am sorry. What is it, do you know?'

'Bees. The vicar's bees.'

'But she wouldn't need to be three, I mean four, days in hospital with a bee sting, surely?'

'Who said she was?'

'What?'

'In hospital for four days. All I said was that she went in Saturday. She come out Saturday too.'

Mrs Pringle took a long draught of tea and looked complacent. She has brought irritating her listeners to a fine art, I'll give her that.

'Well, go on. Tell me it all from the beginning.'

'Mrs Partridge told me herself as she was simply up the

garden picking some nice sprigs of parsley to make parsley sauce for a nice bit of fresh haddock she'd got from that nice fishmonger in Caxley...'

Who probably had a nice shop, I thought impatiently.

'*Miles* away from the hive, she said, when one of the nasty things came and bit her by the eye, and she swelled up awful. Couldn't see out of that eye in a quarter of an hour, and the other not much better, and the vicar looking everywhere for his glasses to read how big a dose of some bee medicine you had to take if bitten – as she had been, of course – and worried to death all the time, in case it was fatal. It can be, you know. My old uncle was never right after being set on by bees, and he died soon after.'

'Really? How dreadful!'

'Mind you, he was ninety-four,' Mrs Pringle admitted, 'but we all said as it was the bee stings as hastened his end. I told the vicar about it.'

Job's comforter, as ever, was my private comment.

'Anyway, she took these tablets, and the vicar got out the car and took her into Caxley Cottage Hospital, and her head was fair swimming by the time she got there. She reckoned it was the medicine. The doctor said it could have been, and give her something to help, and some ointment. She come straight back and went to bed, poor thing, and you can still see where its fangs went into her.'

She heaved herself to her feet.

'Well, I'd best get on. No rest for the wicked, my mother used to say.'

She surveyed my reclining form with a sour expression.

'Though that don't always seem to fit the case, come to think of it.'

After she had returned to the fray, I opened Lucy's letter. It was dated 12 February, which showed how long it had been collecting dust at the back of the dresser.

In it Lucy informed me that Mr and Mrs Ambrose B. Edelstein and their two grown-up children were to be in England for three months. They came from – here an illegible place name, possibly Minnesota, Minever or even Minnehaha – where they took a keen interest in Education, and the Professor had several degrees in the subject. They were such a nice family – I thought of Mrs Pringle – and would be fascinated by a glimpse of Fairacre School, so she had taken the liberty of giving them my telephone number, and they would be ringing me to arrange a convenient day to visit. No need to put them up, or get them meals, as they were planning to stop in Caxley, but she was sure I would enjoy having them in school for a day just letting them have a free rein talking to the children and looking through their work.

She was ever my affectionate Lucy, and added a post-script saying that there was absolutely no need for me to feel that I must reply. I breathed a sigh of relief for mercies received, calculated that the Edelsteins had now been safely back in Minniewhatsit for several months, and fell into a blissful sleep.

Mrs Pringle and the lawnmower man brought me back to earth, half an hour later, and life began anew.

My Norfolk holiday was a great success. There is something about the bracing salty air of that magnificent county, with its massive skies and pellucid light, which is wonderfully restorative. In the summer, that is. I have only once experienced really wintry weather in that area, and hope never to again. Such piercing cold, straight from the steppes of Russia, it seemed, had an intensity never met with in Fairacre, even though we are always telling each other that we live in a cold spot.

On the way to stay with my old friend, and on my return journey, I spent a few hours in Cambridge, so dear to me, and renewed my delight with walks along the Backs, Parker's Piece and Midsummer Common. August is not the best month to see Cambridge, or any other place for that matter, for the trees and grass begin to look worn and shabby, the first glory of summer has gone, and the true fire and radiance of autumn has not begun. But to my devoted eye, there was beauty enough and to spare, and I hung over Clare Bridge and watched the scattered yellow willow leaves floating gently beneath me with the same rapture which I felt in my youth.

There is so little water in Fairacre, and I do not realize how much I miss it until I come across a river, or a lake, or even a modest garden fountain, and experience that surge of joy for this most beautiful of the elements.

But, as always, it was good to get back to my own home. Tibby greeted me with some hauteur. She looked upon my

absence as dereliction of duty, and was not going to put herself out with a lot of fulsome welcoming. Later, if I did the right thing with offerings of rabbit or finely chopped pig's liver, she might condescend to accept me again.

Mrs Pringle had obviously been bottoming me in my absence, and the house shone. She had even put some sweet peas in a vase on the mantelpiece, a gesture which, from one of her morose mood, I much appreciated.

Later, I wrote to my Norfolk friend and decided that it would do me good to walk to the post office. The evening was overcast, and it was sad to see how much shorter the days were growing. Already there were yellow leaves fluttering down from the old plum tree in the garden, and dahlias and Michaelmas daisies were opening in the border. Far too soon, autumn would be upon us and lovely though it always was at Fairacre, with its flaming beech trees and bronzed hedges, yet there was sadness too at the passing of summer and all its outdoor pleasures.

Letter in hand, I opened the front door to find Joan Benson about to thread the Parish Magazine through the letter box.

'Come in,' I cried.

'But you're just going out.'

'Not really. The post's gone anyway, and this will keep till tomorrow.'

'Then I will. I've a stone or something in my shoe, and perhaps I can sit down and investigate.'

It turned out to be a nail, and we had a few minutes of amateurish hammering to try and remedy the matter. We found the activity extremely frustrating, as there was not room enough inside the shoe to manoeuvre the hammer. However, by dint of banging energetically we effected a partial cure.

'We ought to have one of those little anvil things,' said Joan 'with three feet on them. Is it called a cobbler's last?'

I confessed ignorance. 'All I know about a cobbler's last is that he should stick to it,' I said, 'but I never really knew what it meant.'

'Like so many sayings,' agreed Joan, standing up to test her shoe. 'All my eye and Betty Martin, for instance.'

'Or right as a trivet.'

'Or being on tenterhooks. This shoe's fine now, thank you. You could set up as a cobbler, as a side line to teaching, you know.'

'I'll consider it. I might need something to do when I retire.'

'You're not thinking of that yet, surely? Incidentally, will you stay here?'

'I doubt it. By that time I rather think this house and school will be on the market. Any sensible woman would have bought a little place of her own before now, but I'm afraid I've left it a bit late.'

Joan Benson nodded understandingly. 'Well, I can sympathize. This house hunting is so *wearing*. I've had another week with my daughter searching for a suitable home, but the more I look the less I like.'

'What exactly are you looking for?'

'You may well ask! Something with no stairs – a ground-floor flat or a bungalow. But I *must* have a little bit of garden, and ideally it should have some trees, and be the sort of private place where one can sit and ruminate without too many people around. The snag is, of course, that it's virtually impossible to find such a place. Barbara is very anxious for me to have an apartment in an old people's home near her, and lovely though it is – it's an old vicarage with a cedar tree on the lawn and even an old nuttery with Kentish cob nuts – one would be among a score or so of other old people, all individually quite charming I have no doubt, but never *alone*.'

'I can understand how you feel.'

'Do you like your solitude too?'

'It's the breath of life to me,' I confessed. 'Perhaps it's because I am with a crowd all day. All I know is, that to come into this little house and to hear the clock ticking and the cat purring, is sheer bliss to me. I can truthfully say I've never felt lonely in my life.'

'Well, I can't say that,' admitted Joan. 'When you've had a husband and children, and latterly my darling mother, always about the place, then to be alone is – not exactly *frightening*, but definitely *disconcerting*. I suppose the ideal thing would be to find a flat near Barbara so that she could see me frequently, but not have me under her feet. She presses me sometimes to make my home with them, and sometimes when I get back exhausted from house hunting I almost give in. But it would never do. It wouldn't be fair to her, or to the children, or to me, to be honest. Grandchildren are adorable for a time, but it's asking too much to have them with you constantly when you are getting on, and I'm quite sure the same thing applies in reverse.'

She picked up the basket containing the few remaining copies of the parish magazine. 'I must finish my little job. Mrs Partridge usually does it, noble soul, but she's away for a few days. You've heard, I expect, about Holly Lodge?'

'No indeed. I only came back from Norfolk a couple of hours ago, so I haven't caught up with the Fairacre news.'

'I think I've sold it. Henry Mawne asked me if his nephew David and his wife could come and have a look at it. A very nice couple. Do you know them?'

I told her the little about them that I knew.

'Well, they are now trying to sell their own place, which shouldn't be too difficult. Miriam knows them rather better than I do, and the marvellous thing is that they hope Miriam will continue to live in the annexe.'

'She must be very pleased.'

A little frown of worry puckered Joan's brow.

'It is *exactly* what I'd hoped for, and I'm sure it will work out beautifully, but at the moment Miriam is now wondering if they are only being kind, and would really want the annexe for themselves. We've all done our best to persuade her that she need not have such qualms, and as she's such a sensible person I'm sure she will realize that is the truth very soon.'

She began to make her way towards the door.

'Do you sometimes find even the most straightforward people horribly *complicated*?' she asked.

'Frequently,' I replied. 'Perhaps that's why we relish our solitude.'

Reg Thorn and his two young men were now back on the school roof. The dormer window was now recognizable, but still seemed to be giving the three of them a certain amount of trouble. In my innocence, I had imagined that the job might take about three weeks, with perhaps a few more days allowed for bad weather, or difficulty in obtaining parts for it, and so on. But here we were, months later, and still no sign of completion.

I never seemed to be able to catch Reg himself. I would see him in the distance from my kitchen window, but by the time I had walked across to speak to him he had leapt into his van and driven off in a cloud of dust. Dodging irate employers, I guessed, was second nature to him by now.

The young men were fast becoming as evasive, at least in making excuses. One was fair, with fast-receding hair; this seemed sad, as he could not have been much more than twenty-five. The other seemed to be covered in thick black hair: head, beard and chest were one luxuriant growth. Only his dark eyes seemed to be visible among this lushness, and it was he who usually answered my questions. His name was Wayne.

'Well, it's like this, miss. The timber merchant's been closed for the holidays, and when he opened last week he couldn't let us have what we wanted because he'd had a sudden order in from that new estate.'

It all sounded pretty weak to me, but there were any number of excuses, equally futile, that were trotted out in answer to my queries, and I began to give up.

Wayne was a nice young man, anyway, and I half respected his loyalty to Reg Thorn. He told me that he had been with him for four years, and had learnt a lot.

'My dad's in the same trade,' he told me, 'and when he gives up I'll probably take over there.'

'Didn't he want you to work with him?'

'Not my dad! Said he didn't want me under his feet while he could still do a day's work, and got me fixed up with Reg. Better for us both, he said. And anyway, I've promised to carry on when he retires.'

'And will he?'

'Not before he's ninety, I don't suppose. I'll be drawing me pension, I reckon, before he gives up.'

Wayne's father, I thought, seemed worthy of respect.

Term began again in the last week of the month. The children, as always, appeared to have forgotten in six weeks everything they had ever learnt under my tuition, but looked brown and cheerful and ready for the new school year.

Miss Briggs looked equally healthy and almost vivacious. She gave me a large smile when I met her in the playground, and included the two young men on the roof in her affability. The infants welcomed her with affection when we went into school, and one of the smallest presented her with a stick of peppermint rock.

'I got it at Berrisford,' he told her. 'My dad took us there on his day off, and we've kep' it safe on the dresser ever since.'

Miss Briggs thanked him with such obvious gratitude that I thought it would be churlish to point out that it had obviously been sucked at one end.

After all, I told myself, it was the thought that counted, and what were a few germs between friends?

9. September

I always enjoy the early part of the autumn term. The new entrants soon settle down, and it is good to have fresh faces in the infants' room. This year there were four new babies and luckily all were good-natured youngsters who refrained from bawling when their mothers left them, but looked about them, bright-eyed and as inquisitve as squirrels at all these fresh interests.

For the last few years we have tried to let the newcomers visit us for a half-day a week in the preceding term, so that they become familiar with their surroundings.

This has helped enormously when they finally make a start at the beginning of the school year. It is a great strain on a young child to be thrust, not only among large numbers of bigger children, but also into a strange building where each has to find his own clothes peg, his desk, the wash basins and, most important of all, the lavatory.

Miss Briggs seemed much more settled, I thought, and certainly better tempered. No one could call her enthusiastic or charming, but her general demeanour was much more cheerful. This had a good effect on her class, and I supposed that the change in attitude resulted from the mellowing influence of the unknown young man, and also the fact that she now felt more confident in her work after two terms of teaching. She was far readier too, I was relieved to see, to remain after school when needed. Quite often she did not go until Reg Thorn's workmen finished at four-thirty, and seemed glad to take on extra little jobs connected with the coming celebrations.

Things were going well in that direction. Mrs Moffat invited me to see Linda's Victorian dress, and I accompanied her from the butcher's where we had met one Saturday morning.

In the room set aside for her sewing, there hung her latest masterpiece. It was a perfect replica of Miss Richards's frock of the early 1880s, as dimly seen in a faded photograph I had found among the school records.

It was made of black woollen crêpe, complete with bustle, and draped over a pleated underskirt of black satin. At the neck was a ruffle of white lace, and embedded in the snowy froth was a beautiful jet brooch.

I exclaimed with admiration.

'Well, it's mostly bits and pieces,' she said modestly, though obviously pleased at my reaction.

'The black material is from an evening frock of mine. The satin was a skirt lining, and the lace I had by me. The bustle is made of foam rubber – much more comfortable than the original horse hair, I should think.'

'And that lovely brooch?'

'My grandmother's. It was the mourning brooch she bought when her father died. She also had a pretty little mourning ring made from his signet ring, but it was lost not long afterwards.'

'Well, Linda's going to be the belle of the ball on this occasion,' I said, stroking the costume.

'Don't be too sure! I think young Patrick will run her pretty close. I've been helping his mother make a serge suit with knee breeches – Norfolk style, you know – and with an Eton collar and bow tie he's going to look absolutely splendid. The only difficulty is persuading Patrick that he won't look what he terms "a proper sissy" in it.'

'I'll work on that problem,' I promised her as I took my leave.

*

Mrs Pringle arrived at school one morning looking un-usually militant. I soon learnt the cause.

'That niece of mine, that Minnie, that *awful* Minnie!'

She gulped with fury, slapping viciously at a desk with her duster.

My heart sank. Minnie Pringle, still known by that name although she is a married woman, is the mother of several children, most of them illegitimate. In a weak moment I once engaged her as a second charwoman, and the havoc she managed to wreak in my house had to be seen to be believed. Whatever had happened to Minnie, I decided now, nothing would persuade me to have her in my home again.

'What has she done?' I ventured to ask her irate aunt.

'She's been and left her Ern, that's what. Had some sort of tiff last night, and up and left him with all those kids.'

'You mean she left the children with Ern?'

'No, no, no! I wish she had! She's brought 'em all up to our place, and I've left her grizzling over the corn flakes. I've told her straight she's to go back to Ern as soon as she's got breakfast down 'em.'

'What went wrong, do you think?'

'Well, you know our Min as well as I do. She's come across that chap Bert again, as she was sweet on once.'

I remembered that Bert was the man who had taken up his abode in their house at Springbourne. Rather naturally Ern had resented it, and there had been ructions.

'But surely Bert got a job elsewhere?'

'Only laying gas pipes. He soon got done with that and made a pretty penny too at it. Now he's having a rest on the Social Security, and you know what they says about Satan finding work for idle hands to do? Well, he's found some with our Min, and Ern's cutting up rough.'

At this moment Eileen Burton rushed in to ask if she

could pull the school bell 'as it wasn't fair the boys always done it'.

I was too surprised by this passionate plea on behalf of equality for women to correct her grammar, and agreed to her request.

Meanwhile Mrs Pringle, limping heavily, had taken herself into the infants' room to continue her onslaught on the furniture, and I shelved Minnie Pringle's problems to face my own.

We were having a spell of unsettled weather. Two days would be calm and golden and the farmers would be wreathed in smiles as they fetched home the last of the harvest, or busily baled the golden straw. Then two or three days of rain would follow, drenching the straw awaiting collection, and filling our playground with extensive puddles which positively challenged the naughtier children to play 'Splashem' in defiance of my veto on the game.

I had just dashed across the playground through a shower at the end of afternoon school, when the telephone rang. Elizabeth Mawne was calling.

'I'm begging a favour,' she began.

'Fire away.'

'Well, I know you often go to Caxley on a Saturday morning, and I wondered if you could give me a lift. I'm going to Jenner's to pick up a christening mug – the christening is the next day and Jenner's have kept me in suspense all this time. Our car's out of order, or I wouldn't bother you.'

I said that I should be delighted, particularly as I had a clock which had been waiting to be mended for quite six months, and I too would visit Jenner's with her.

By half-past ten on Saturday we were on our way, splashing through the streaming lanes on one of the wettest days of our changeable spell.

'It really is annoying,' said Mrs Mawne. 'All my roses are turning brown with the rain, and I am doing the church flowers this Sunday and was relying on roses for my arrangements. The most reliable flowers in the garden at the moment are marigolds. Perhaps not quite right for church decoration.'

'Why not? Everyone likes them, and they always look so cheerful. I'd plump for the marigolds every time.'

'Perhaps I will,' agreed Mrs Mawne, but she sounded doubtful. There is no gainsaying, I thought, that the ladies who take their flower-arranging seriously store up a mint of trouble for themselves one way or another.

'You've heard that David hopes to move into Holly Lodge?'

I said that I had.

'Henry was so grateful to you for advising him. He gets into rather a tizzy over things like that.'

'But I did nothing,' I protested.

'You let him *bumble on* to you,' said his wife. 'It helped. He rang David straightaway, and he and Irene think it is exactly what they want. David can go to town by train quite easily, or on the motorway. He'll have to get a second car, but there we are. It will be good to have them at hand, and it will be so much healthier for them all, particularly for Simon. He's a frail child.'

I thought of the strength which had gone into the hurling of that quoit which had killed our dear albino robin, but said nothing.

'Of course, Joan Benson has to find somewhere, and David is still advertising his place, but we hope the move can be made well before Christmas. At a pinch, they can move in with us temporarily, but we hope it won't come to that. It wouldn't please *any* of us, and between ourselves, I think poor Henry would go mad.'

I jammed on the brakes to avoid a suicidal pheasant who

strutted with great dignity and deliberation across the road in front of us.

'Of course,' continued Elizabeth, when we drove on, 'you are so lucky having a place of your own. I imagine you will stay on there when you retire?'

I explained my position.

'So what will you do? I hadn't realized that the school-house was virtually a tied cottage.'

'Oh, something will turn up,' I said with a cheerfulness I did not feel. 'Well, here we are, and miracles will never cease! There's actually a parking place.'

Jenner's is an old-fashioned shop, run in earlier times by the widow of the original jeweller, Edward Jenner. Although she is now bedridden, her two sons who run the business consult her over every transaction in the shop, which is somewhat trying if you are in a hurry.

Sometimes a good bellow up the stairs suffices. A faint reply is vaguely heard by the customer, and one of the sons returns to cope with the matter, fortified by mother's help. But today, Mrs Mawne and I had to wait while John Jenner pounded up the stairs holding two christening mugs.

Time passed. We shifted from one foot to the other, and studied barometers, clocks, wrist watches, dress rings, engagement rings, babies' spoons and pushers, rose bowls, and innumerable candlesticks.

It was obvious that Elizabeth was growing even more impatient than I was. She has not had to put up with waiting for others, and is extremely forthright in her speech when crossed. I wondered what sort of welcome John Jenner would get on his return. Elizabeth's foot was tapping dangerously when he appeared at last.

'Your mother, Mr Jenner,' she said severely, 'reminds me of the Almighty. Invisible and omnipotent.'

'She's all of that,' agreed John Jenner.

*

Determined though I was not to get mixed up in Minnie Pringle's matrimonial squalls, yet nevertheless I found myself unwillingly involved.

She arrived one day in the following week with three of her brood to see if they could attend Fairacre School while she was 'with auntie'. There was not much I could do about it, and so I agreed with as much grace as I could muster.

I handed the three into the charge of Linda Moffat, who is a kind motherly child with plenty of sense. She undertook to show them where to hang their coats, and so on.

Meanwhile, Minnie showed no desire to leave my presence. The children were still out in the playground as it was only twenty to nine. Miss Briggs had not yet arrived, and so had no inkling of two new infants to be added – temporarily, I trusted – to her roll. The eldest child would be with me.

Minnie looked as much like a scarecrow as she had always done. Her ankle-length frock must once have been an evening dress. Over it she wore a thick ribbed pullover which had half a dozen grimy badges tacked on to it. Her bare feet were thrust into broken peep-toe sandals of scarlet plastic material, and her red hair was as unkempt as a well-used floor mop.

A young baby was asleep under the hood of the battered pram in the lobby, and a toddler with a repellently runny nose sat at the other end. With five children under nine one could not help but feel sorry for poor silly Minnie, but I steeled myself to withstand any offers of renewed housework. I had suffered enough in the past.

'You heard about my Ern?' she enquired.

I said guardedly that Mrs Pringle had said that he had left home.

'Ah! But did she tell you where he'd gone?'

'No.'

'Back to that Mrs Fowler in Caxley!'

Minnie spoke triumphantly, as though she had scored a point. Frankly, I was flummoxed. An earlier union between the renowned Mrs Fowler and Minnie's Ern had ended in such acrimony that I should have thought that they would never see each other again.

'She's been at him for months to go back as a lodger. Misses the money, see? Well, now he's gone.'

'Just like that? He must have had a reason.'

Minnie hesitated, running her dirty fingernails through her equally dirty locks. She seemed to be struggling with a desire to tell me all.

It won.

'I don't mind you knowing, but Ern got a bit nasty about Bert popping in, and he took his belt to me. Then Bert got wild and clocked him one, so Ern cleared off, and the language what he used I wouldn't tell a lady like you. Real *rude*, it was! Animals and that!'

'But where will you live? I believe the house is in your name, isn't it?'

'That's right. But I'm feared of sleeping there alone in case Ern comes back.'

'I should certainly move back as soon as you can,' I advised her, thinking of myself as much as Minnie, I don't mind admitting. 'The council won't want the place empty, and I gather your aunt can't have you there.'

'She don't seem very pleased about it,' agreed Minnie, taking a grubby handkerchief to the toddler's nose, and not before time. 'I'll be all right. I'm going to get Bert to sleep in until Ern comes back.'

She gave me her wide demented smile and pushed the pram out of the lobby.

'I'll be all right,' echoed in my brain for most of the day. Inconsistent, crazy, immoral, come to think of it, there was no doubt that Minnie would emerge from this little battle quite unscathed. It would be the non-belligerents, encountered on the way, who would be scarred.

Amy called to see me one blustery afternoon. She had brought me the latest collection of Flora Thompson's writings as a present, and as a lover of *Lark Rise to Candleford* I could hardly wait to begin *A Country Calendar*.

'You spoil me,' I told her.

'I know. You can give me a cup of tea in exchange.'

'And where have you been?' I asked, as I warmed the teapot.

'Oxford. Bumbling round Blackwell's in a happy daze, and spending far too much money. I tell myself I am getting Christmas presents, but I know damn well I shan't be able to part with any of them.'

'Never mind. Think how it boosts trade.'

'Mind you, I did get a splendid eiderdown for the spare room, but can you guess what it's called?'

'Not a clue.'

'Well, wait for it. On the label it says: *Morsnugga*!'

'I don't believe it.'

'I'd show you if I could be bothered to unwrap it, you doubting Thomas! For two pins, I would have given it back, but it was the only one which was the right colour, and I only hope my visitors will sleep too soundly to want to read eiderdown labels. But I ask you – *Morsnugga*! It really is the end, isn't it?'

'It could have been something with "cosy" in it, spelt with a "K".'

'That's true. This is a first-class cup of tea. I can well do with it. Shopping creases me these days, and I used to enjoy it.'

'How's the book getting on?'

'It isn't. I'm still aged eight, and I honestly don't think I can go on. It seems a pity. I've done about eight thousand words, and the thought of doing another fifty or sixty, which is what is needed, I gather, for a book's length, is too daunting for words.'

'Can't you do something with the bit you've done? Make a magazine article, say, or a talk for the radio?'

Amy looked thoughtful. 'That's an idea. I could make something of being a Brownie half a century ago, and there's quite a nice episode about my mother opening a flower show when the marquee collapsed.'

'It all sounds good clean fun to me,' I told her, refilling her tea cup. 'You have a bash. You can't waste all that effort.'

'I agree. Do you know, I sometimes think you are more intelligent than you look.'

'Thank you, Amy,' I said. 'I shall treasure that remark.'

The wind was more violent than ever when Amy departed. Branches clashed overhead, plants shuddered in the onslaught, and a weird hooting came from the television aerial as the wind whistled around it.

Tibby rushed in through the front door as I waved farewell to Amy. She looked startled and affronted. I had little sympathy for her as she can get into shelter through the cat flap on the back door, but this is beneath her dignity if anyone is about to open a proper door for the lady.

It was good to get indoors again. I cleared away our tea things, put aside a pile of exercise books due to be corrected, and settled down gleefully with my lovely new book. After twenty minutes' bliss, a strange sound became evident. It was difficult to pin-point just what and just where it was in the confusion of noises outside, but to my horror it sounded remarkably like heavy breathing.

A burglar, with bronchitis? But he would hardly be at his work in such a condition. An escaped lunatic? But our nearest asylum was some twenty miles away. Some poor traveller taken ill and needing my assistance? If my conjecture was correct, he would need a doctor and oxygen tent immediately.

It was all very unnerving. The longer I listened, the more sure I became that it really was breathing that I could hear. What on earth should I do? It is on occasions like this that I realize how useful a husband could be. How lovely to be able to say: 'I think someone is breaking in, dear,' and to settle back while a masculine hand raises the poker.

However, spinsters learn to cope alone, and I decided that I must go and investigate. Tibby remained quite unmoved by the noise, which was unusual. Anything strange often causes her to growl, and to bristle with fright or fury, which only adds to one's misgivings.

I took the poker in hand, and went to the front door, switching on lights as I went. Outside, grazing peacefully among my herbaceous plants was a fine Guernsey cow, one of Mr Roberts's herd, I guessed. By the light from the hall I caught sight of my lawn, heavily indented by hoofs, and wondered what Mr Willet would have to say about his newly mown grass when he turned up next morning.

The cow gazed benignly at me, some choice penstemon flowers dangling from her rotating jaw. She seemed pleased to see me, and made a gentle lowing noise through her mouthful of light supper.

Much relieved – for who would not prefer a kindly, if hungry cow to an escaped madman? – I rang Mr Roberts's number and awaited rescue.

As I had guessed, Mr Willet was most indignant when he saw the state of my lawn the next morning.

'Never saw such a muck-up in all my borns,' he said, blowing out his moustache with disgust. 'You wants to sue old Roberts. That animal's done pounds' worth of damage.'

'I can't do that,' I protested. 'It's one of the hazards of living in the country. Cows do get out sometimes.'

'Not if the fences is kept proper,' replied Mr Willet sternly. 'Well, if you won't do nothing, you won't, of course, but I shall tell him what I think when I comes across him next.'

'Oh, don't make trouble!' I begged him. 'If I don't mind why should you?'

'Because I shall have the rolling and flattening of this lot, I can see, that's why!'

Against such straight reasoning I could say nothing, but made my way to school.

Here more trouble awaited me. Water had blown through the half-finished dormer window and made a pool on the floor. Joseph Coggs was doing his best to mop it up, but in his zeal was using Mrs Pringle's new duster and I foresaw some ructions.

'Let me have that, Joseph,' I said snatching it from him, 'and get the old floor cloth from the lobby.'

I was wondering if I could tear home, and put the duster to dry out of Mrs Pringle's sight, when the lady arrived, and caught me duster-handed.

'And who,' she boomed, 'done that?'

'It was used in error,' I said placatingly. 'One of the children was mopping up and didn't realize –'

At this moment, Joseph appeared with the floor cloth and Mrs Pringle rounded on him before I could intervene.

'You use my dusters once more, young Joe, and you'll get my hand round your ear-hole! Understand?'

Poor Joe turned pale. Mrs Pringle has hands like hams, and it was no idle threat.

'You can leave the cloth with me, Joseph,' I said hastily, 'and go into the playground until the bell goes.'

I mustered all the dignity I could manage whilst dangling a wet rag in each hand.

'I will see to this,' I said coldly, 'and please don't bully the children.'

Mrs Pringle grabbed the duster and shook it violently. 'You can do what you like with that floor cloth,' she shouted, 'but I'm not trusting you with my nice new duster.'

With that she thrust the damp duster into her black oilcloth bag, presumably to be taken home for its correct treatment, and I was left to mop the floor and curse Mrs Pringle, dormer windows, the wind, and Reg Thorn with equal intensity.

Miss Briggs arrived half an hour late with laryngitis. She had had a puncture, luckily in Beech Green, she whispered painfully, and two of Mr Annett's big boys had changed the wheel for her.

I went into the infants' room with her to supply their wants, and to tell them of their teacher's affliction and the necessity for exemplary behaviour. It was going to be one of those days, I thought grimly, as Wayne switched on his transistor set overhead and filled the air with discord.

As it happened, with Miss Briggs's normally stentorian tones now hushed, it was the quietest day at Fairacre school since her arrival.

The rough weather had done some damage in our area. A tarpaulin had blown from a newly built stack of straw and caught itself in a neighbouring plum tree, bringing down several laden branches.

A branch had crashed on Henry Mawne's greenhouse, and rumour had it that the vicar had gone in his pyjamas to make sure that his beehives were safe.

In my own garden, the cow had done more damage than the weather, but the television aerial was sloping at an extraordinary angle.

'I can fix that, miss,' Wayne assured me. 'Just got to straighten one of the window catches, and then I'll be there.'

The dormer window, so Reg Thorn said, when I was successful in catching him one morning, would be finished in a fortnight.

'Just a final coat of paint, and we won't be bothering you

no more,' he told me with pride. 'How d'you think it looks?'

'Fine,' I said, gazing at the new structure. To be honest, I was not sure about it. It looked heavy and awkward, jutting out from the old roof, but I was so used to the unobtrusive line of the old skylight that anything different was bound to strike me as peculiar. Mr Willet's derogatory remarks too may have influenced me. In any case, the new window must surely be an improvement on the former one which had plagued all the inhabitants of Fairacre school for generations.

Wayne put my aerial to rights as he promised and I thanked him at playtime.

'Don't you mind heights?' I asked him.

'Enjoy 'em,' he said beaming. 'My uncle was a steeplejack. Used to scramble up factory chimneys and walk round the rim at the top.'

To hear about it made me feel queasy.

'No good being a builder unless you've got the stomach for heights,' said Wayne, carrying Reg Thorn's ladder back to its proper place.

The children came out of school to play, and I was thankful that sunshine had followed the stormy weather. Miss Briggs emerged too to take up her playground duty, and Wayne hurried over to talk to her. It was good to see her so friendly and animated, I thought. She would miss the young company when our dormer window was done at last.

The Pringle children were still with us and much as I wanted to know what Minnie's plans were – if any – I was anxious not to appear too curious by asking Mrs Pringle about conditions at her home. However, she appeared one morning with a nasty scratch down one cheek and a large lump on her forehead.

'Good lord, Mrs Pringle,' I exclaimed, 'have you had a fall?'

'No. But someone else has,' she told me with enormous satisfaction.

She settled herself on the front desk, her usual perch when about to give me all the news. I glanced anxiously at the clock. No need to ring the school bell yet, and although I had still to look out the morning hymn and open the windows, it seemed far more important to me to hear the story behind Mrs Pringle's injuries.

'Well, it's like this. That Minnie wouldn't do nothing about getting Ern back as long as Bert was around and she could see him. I threatened to put her and the kids out in the road, but you know our Min. Water off a duck's back it was, and me going half-barmy with that lot under my feet.'

'But I thought Ern worked at Springbourne Manor. Didn't the Potters wonder where he was when he didn't turn up?'

'That's just it! He *did* turn up! Come on the bus from Caxley each morning, so the Potters never twigged anything was wrong for some time. But, of course, someone tittle-tattled to Mr Potter, and he waylaid Bert, as he sacked for pinching the vegetables if you remember, and got the truth out of him about Minnie and Ern.'

'What happened?'

'He ticked off Bert, and told him not to come between husband and wife, and to keep out of Springbourne or he'd set the police on him. Then he come up our place the other day and had a good talking to Minnie. He told her that Ern would lose his job if she didn't persuade him to go back to live in Springbourne.'

'And did she?'

'Not Minnie! She's a proper soft one! Said Ern might hit her and she was scared, though if he promised to treat her right she might go back. I said to her: "If you won't persuade Ern, then I will, my girl! I've had enough of you and your brats eating me out of house and home, and using my sheets and towels, day in and day out!" So yesterday evening I went to Caxley, and sorted things out.'

She fingered the bump on her head with pride. I was mightily impressed at the thought of even such a doughty fighter as Mrs Pringle facing the formidable Mrs Fowler. She once lived in Fairacre, and was a tough shrewish woman who frightened the life out of me just to look at her.

'You went to Mrs Fowler's?'

'I did indeed. She started shouting before I'd hardly got the words out of my mouth about Ern. "You let me in and we can talk this over nicely," I said to her, but what she said in return I wouldn't sully my lips by repeating. She made a run at me and that's when I got this scratch, the spiteful cat.'

'Did you retaliate?'

'If you mean did I give her as good as I got, I certainly did. Two handfuls of her hair I tore out, and I blacked her eye.'

Mrs Pringle spoke with quiet satisfaction. It must have been a real battle of the dinosaurs, I thought, and I wondered if the neighbours had enjoyed it.

'She said Ern wasn't there, but down The Barleycorn, and what's more he spent all his time there. Then she slammed the door in my face. I was about to go off to the pub to see if she was telling the truth, when she opened a top window and chucked a suitcase at me, with Ern's things in evidently. Anyway, that's what caused this bump – not that woman.'

At this juncture, Joseph Coggs put his head round the door to say was it time for the bell, and could he ring it?

'Not just yet, Joe. Mrs Pringle and I are having a little talk. I'll call you in a few minutes.'

Joseph vanished.

'Go on! Was he there?'

'He was. I picked up the case and went round the corner and found him in the bar. We just had time to get the last bus back.'

'He came without any trouble?' I asked mystified.

'I *took him*,' said Mrs Pringle.

I gazed at her with respect.

Outside I could hear the sound of children's voices. Were my latest pupils among them? I asked my cleaner.

'They're all going back to Springbourne tonight. Mr Potter's lending Ern the van to fetch the lot, and told him straight that he's out on his ear if he don't treat our Minnie right.'

'And you think he will behave now?'

'If he don't,' said Mrs Pringle rising majestically, 'he knows there's *two* of us can settle him.'

She made her way into the lobby, and I called Joseph in to ring the bell, some five minutes after time.

Meanwhile, I looked out the morning hymn, and settled for *Fight the Good Fight*, as an appropriate choice in the circumstances.

10. *October*

Oddly enough, I heard more about the clashing of the monsters from Amy when she visited me a few days later. Her window cleaner lives next door to Mrs Fowler in Caxley, and he evidently gave her a lively description of the scene.

'He and his wife went upstairs to get a better view from the bedroom window,' Amy told me. 'And whatever Mrs P. may say to the contrary, her language was quite as lurid as Mrs Fowler's. He said their money was on Mrs Pringle right from the start. "She'd got the *motive* and the *spirit* and the *weight*!" was how he put it.'

'Very neatly put too. They must have made an unholy noise. It's a wonder the neighbours didn't call the police.'

'They were enjoying it so much I don't think they wanted to break it up. According to him, it was pretty plain that Ern was getting fed up at Mrs Fowler's anyway. She used to expect him to do all the odd jobs around the house when he got back from Springbourne, and the food was rather sparse, I gather.'

'I can well believe that! Mrs Fowler had the reputation of being the stingiest woman in Fairacre when she lived here.'

'So it looks as though Ern was ripe for the picking, and Mrs P. plucked him at the right moment.'

'Well, heaven bless the old harridan,' I said. 'Now we've seen the last of Minnie and her brood.'

'For a time, anyway,' Amy said. 'I've no doubt they'll turn up in your life again before long.'

'Heaven forbid! Tell me, how's the dismemberment of the book going?'

Amy looked quite animated. 'I sent two short episodes to *Woman's Hour* and they've taken one. I'm going up to broadcast it, probably early next year.'

'Marvellous! We'll have it on at school in the afternoon. Tell me more.'

'Well, I'm writing an account of our sick room at school.'

'It sounds somewhat morbid.'

'Not really. It's supposed to be rather funny. You've no idea how dreadfully depressing that place was. It's doing me good to write it out of my system.'

'What was wrong with it?'

'Everything! For one thing, it was a symphony in green, of all colours.'

'Very restful, they say.'

'Not when you're bilious, as most of the inmates were. And the greens didn't harmonize, to make it worse. And the only decoration was a past pupil's lettering exercise in the most excruciating calligraphy, quite impossible to read from one's sick bed, but it was evidently that passage from Chaucer about the poor scholar who had twenty books clad in black and red. What with the writing and the spelling, one could feel one's mind giving way.'

'You should have closed your eyes.'

'Even so you were assailed by the most nauseating smell of something the mistress who had attended you burnt on an enamel plate on the floor. It was called Persian tape, if I remember rightly, and if you weren't sick when you arrived you pretty soon were once the Persian tape got going.'

'Were you allowed visitors?'

'Only the odd relative. Anyway, this ghastly place was at the very top of a high building, and most people jibbed at all the stairs. Patients were always in a state of collapse when they finally arrived, with their knees like jelly.'

'Well, I hope you can do justice to it,' I said. 'It sounds as though you have plenty of material.'

'It should do something for my suppressed emotions anyway,' said Amy, with evident satisfaction. 'Now tell me your news. How's the centenary programme going?'

'I'm having Linda and Patrick over here after school tomorrow to try them out with their lines. Miss Clare, bless her, needs no rehearsing, nor Mrs Austen, and Mr Lamb from the post office has promised to tell us something about the famous trip to Wembley in the 1920s. It's not going to be such a formidable job as I first thought, and Miss Briggs is being unusually helpful with the singing.'

'Do you think she'll stay?'

'I'm beginning to hope so. She's much more cheerful since she found that young man, and she's gradually forgetting a lot of the high-falutin' rubbish she was stuffed with at college, thank heaven.'

'Well, good luck with it all,' said Amy, collecting her things. 'By the way, James and I are having a short break in Wales next week to make up for his missing Tresco in the summer, so I shan't see you for a time.'

'Do you know, I thought I might go again next summer to Tresco. I loved it so much.'

'Then book up early,' advised Amy. 'We're going again, but in May, when you'll be hard at work, of course, and we've already staked our claim.'

'It seems rather soon,' I said, 'to book for August.'

'*You do it now*!' replied Amy sternly. 'What a terrible procrastinator you are! I wonder anything *ever* gets done in this establishment. Now mind! Sit down and write to that hotel this evening.'

'Yes, Amy,' I said meekly.

I had written the simplest possible dialogue for Linda as Miss Richards, and for Patrick as the bad boy John

Pratt, but even so they seemed to find it difficult to memorize.

'Don't worry if it's not exactly the same,' I implored them. 'As long as you get the meaning across, that's all that matters.'

If anything, this confused them even more. We had a break, and I produced lemonade and biscuits. Tibby entered and received a great deal of admiration from the two, and then we resumed. After two or three attempts, things went more smoothly. Linda seemed to be less self-conscious than Patrick and with practice I thought the little scene should go well.

'We'll try it with the other children one day this week,' I promised them, 'and by that time you'll know your lines so well, it will be much easier to concentrate on the movements.'

They looked doubtful, and I must confess that if these two comparatively bright pupils made such heavy weather of their parts, it did not look too hopeful for the rest of my cast. Again I felt thankful that most of the performances would be in the more capable hands of three or more adults.

They departed clutching their two-page scripts with them, their young brows furrowed with anxiety. Perhaps I was expecting too much from them, I thought, as I waved them good-bye? Fairacre children are shy by nature, and perhaps the idea of displaying their modest talents in front of parents and, even worse, their schoolfellows, was going to prove too much for their nerves.

We could only wait and see.

As so often happens in October, the weather was balmy, the skies cloudless, and that clear light peculiar to a fine autumn bathed Fairacre in end-of-summer beauty.

The hedges were bright with glossy berries. The trees

were beginning to blaze in all shades of yellow, bronze and crimson, and the cottage gardens, so far untouched by frost, were still gay with asters, Michaelmas daisies, chrysanthemums and dahlias.

I relish these sparkling autumn days, all the more keenly because one knows that there cannot be many of them before waking one morning to a hoary scene and the knowledge that winter has arrived. I took the children out for plenty of exhilarating walks on the downs, and after tea each day walked again on my own before the sun set. By six o'clock it was beginning to grow chilly, and I enjoyed lighting a fire and congratulating myself on having the best of both worlds while the fine spell lasted.

On one of my solitary walks, through a little copse at the foot of the downs, I came across Miriam Quinn who was enjoying the fresh air as much as I was, to judge by her pink cheeks and bright eyes. We walked along together in great content.

'This is the breath of life to me,' she said, 'after the office. I look forward to it all day. Caxley's all very well for working, but I simply couldn't go back there to live after Fairacre.'

'You're not proposing to, are you?' I asked.

She looked thoughtful, bending down to remove a briar which had caught her skirt.

'No. I'm staying, and I hope I'm doing the right thing. You know the young Mawnes are taking over?'

I said that Joan had told me.

'Well, I still have slight doubts about whether they truly want me living under the same roof. They've been terribly kind, and pressed me to stay, and as I honestly can't find a thing worth considering elsewhere, I have agreed. In any case, I love it here, as you know, and it would be a dreadful wrench to have to leave.'

'I'm sure they really do want you to stay. Henry Mawne was relieved to know you would be there when David was away on his business trips. I remember him saying how comforting it would be for Irene to have company in the house at night.'

'Really?' Miriam sounded pleased but slightly incredulous. 'I hadn't thought of that. I must say, it's nice to be useful. I have already offered to sit with young Simon in the holidays if they want to go out in the evening. Irene seemed pleased about that, which delighted me.'

'It would help them enormously, I'm sure.'

We walked along in silence for a short time, until we emerged into one of Mr Roberts's fields, and turned towards the village. Miriam seemed to be turning over my remarks in her mind.

'You know,' she said at last, 'one of the difficulties of being single is that there is no one to discuss these little problems with. It's so easy to see just one's own point of view. I'm glad you told me about Henry Mawne's comment. Of course, he's quite right. I'm afraid I've been far too self-centred over all this business – anxious not to intrude, anxious about finding somewhere else, in fact, thoroughly steamed up and not really thinking of Irene and David's side of the problem. That must be one of the bonuses of married life, I imagine – being able to share one's troubles.'

'Except that you've got two people's troubles then,' I pointed out. 'Think how relatively uncomplicated our spinsterhood is!'

Miriam stopped in her tracks and laughed aloud. It was good to see her usually pensive expression replaced by joyous animation. She ought to laugh more often, I thought.

'Perhaps you're right. Anyway, I'm glad we met in the wood. I'm going home in a much more cheerful state of mind. What about coming back to Holly Lodge for a drink?'

'I'd love to,' I said, and we stepped out briskly together.

The vicar called in to school one gloriously sunny afternoon, and we enthused about the weather. He is as devoted to the sun as I am, and when the rest of the villagers are collapsing with heat, he and I gloat together on perfect conditions for sun-worshippers.

He bore a jar of his own honey, and presented it to me with considerable pride. I thanked him sincerely, and enquired after the bees.

'They've really done splendidly. I collected about sixty pounds of honey. It's so rewarding to see it pouring out of the extractor in a beautiful golden stream. To think that those dear bees have made thousands and thousands of trips, all through the summer, to collect the delicious stuff from all our beautiful Fairacre flowers!'

Obviously, our vicar was enraptured.

'Are they still about?'

'Yes, indeed! As busy as ever. I think they are collecting from the bramble flowers and willow herb now. I don't propose to take any more. What they fetch in now will help them through the winter.'

'Is there much for you to do to prepare them for the cold weather?'

'A *great deal*,' said he earnestly. 'They will need some sugar syrup, and I intend to put up the mouse guards at the entrances. They creep in, you know, for shelter, and possibly the honey. Quite alarming for the bees. I shall certainly take steps to protect them from marauders.'

He took a slip of paper from his pocket and consulted it.

'A quarter of mushrooms, half of tomatoes, a dozen large eggs – no, that isn't it.'

He turned over the paper.

'Ah! Here we are, on the back of my wife's shopping list, you see. First of all, how is the new window?'

'So far, so good,' I told him.

'That's fine. Really, the old skylight was a sore trial when the weather was rough. We should have a snug winter with this new one.'

I said I hoped so.

'Then the next thing I have here is to fix a date for the centenary service.'

He lowered the paper and looked unhappy. 'I rather think I shall have to combine it with a Sunday service in

December. My diary has suddenly become horribly full for that month. What do you think? I thought perhaps the Sunday before Christmas might be suitable. It would be the last Sunday of term, and we could have prayers and hymns suitable to the occasion at morning service, and my sermon would be on the subject of our heritage here in the village.'

'It sounds ideal,' I said, 'and the church would be looking festive too by that stage.'

'Certainly,' said the vicar looking mightily relieved at my amiability. What did he expect, I wondered? That I might fling myself to the floor, screaming and drumming my heels?

'The crib would certainly be in place, and no doubt some of the Christmas greenery. Perhaps we could arrange for the children to do some of the decorations, as they do for Harvest Festival?'

'That's a nice idea,' I said, but had private reservations about how the flower ladies would react to juvenile assistance at Christmas time.

'Good, good!' said Mr Partridge, making for the door. 'I really ought to have a bonfire, I've so much garden stuff to burn, but I intend to wait until dusk. Nothing is going to detract from this beautiful sunshine if I can help it.'

'A case of "Gather ye rosebuds while ye may",' I quoted.

'Absolutely, Miss Read. Absolutely!'

He looked at the children with his usual benevolence.

'I should take them for a walk this afternoon,' he whispered confidentially.

'Don't worry,' I told him. 'It's at the head of the agenda.'

11. November

It was a relief to be without Minnie Pringle's three children. Not that they were naughty or rumbustious. In fact, they were just the opposite, and sat immobile in their desks contributing nothing and, as far as one could see, taking in nothing.

They were all mouth-breathers, which was hardly surprising considering the revolting state of their nasal passages, and no amount of advice, persuasion or example succeeded in showing them how to blow their noses. They were like their mother in being almost unteachable, but without her demented energy. What they would do when it came to earning a living I shuddered to think. No doubt an indulgent welfare state would give them far more for doing nothing than they were capable of earning anyway.

But if I were relieved to see the back of Minnie's brood, I was really sorry to say farewell to the shepherd's children. Perhaps he had found a better job than his new one with Mr Roberts?

Mr Willet enlightened me.

'Bin pinchin'. Not just the odd egg or swede and that. He done in one of Mr Roberts's sheep, and sold it to that back-street butcher in Caxley. Ought to be deported, the pair of 'em, but I don't suppose they'll get more than probation when the case comes up.'

'Well, they certainly won't get deported,' I assured Mr Willet. 'Anyway, who'd want them?'

'We don't, that's for sure! And Mr Roberts is hopping mad. Now he's got to start all over again getting some new chap. Can't trust a soul these days, Miss Read. They'd take your teeth off the table if you was fool enough to leave 'em there.'

'At the moment,' I told him, 'my teeth – what are left of them – don't take out.'

Mr Willet looked sympathetic.

'Then you've a mort of trouble ahead of you. I'm thankful to say all mine are national gnashers now, and it's a great comfort to be able to take 'em out now and again to give me gums a nice airing.'

He set out across the playground, and then turned.

'Bring the numbers down a bit though, won't it? Them Pringle kids and shepherd's lot? Bet you'll be hearing from the office.'

'Oh, shut up,' I begged him.

For the horrid fact was much in my mind too.

Another cause for relief was the absence of Reg Thorn's men. I had grown quite fond of them both, and found Wayne particularly sensible and friendly. Nevertheless, it was wonderful to be free of that everlasting cacophony from their transistor radio, and from the bangs and thumps as they worked overhead.

Mr Willet still looked askance at the finished product, but as I pointed out, no rain had come through now that it was completed, and we certainly seemed to have more light.

'Hasn't had a fair test yet,' Mr Willet warned me. 'You wait till that old wind gets up!'

Unfortunately, we did not have to wait long. The halcyon October weather broke early in November with lashing rain and a high wind.

I was relieved to see that no water came through, as it certainly would have done in the old days, but there was an annoying drumming sound as the wind caught the jutting framework. I was not too happy about this vibration, and rang Reg Thorn during the dinner hour. For once he was at home.

'I've got to come over to Springbourne this afternoon,' he told me. 'I'll pop in on my way.'

As one might expect, the wind had dropped considerably by the time he arrived, and the drumming was hardly in evidence. Nevertheless, he clambered up to the window and seemed to make a fairly exhaustive study of the structure.

'Right as a trivet,' he assured me when he descended. 'Good bit of work that! You don't need to worry about a thing. Them boys of mine know what they're up to. By the way, have you heard about Ted Richards?'

I looked blank. 'Do I know him?'

'Young Wayne's dad. He's had a stroke. The boy's off work for a few days, helping out.'

'I'm sorry to hear that. How's the old man getting on?'

'Pretty well. His speech is back, and the doctor says his arm is coming round. Shook the old boy though. I reckon I'll be losing Wayne, and I'll be sorry. He's a good worker, and a bit more up top than some I could mention. Still, his dad comes first, I can see that.'

He stepped back to take a last satisfied look at his creation, and then departed.

I woke in the night to the howling of a terrific gale. I could hear a door banging downstairs, and got out of bed to go and shut it. As I did so a horrific rumbling sounded overhead, and I guessed that a tile had blown loose and was bumping down the roof.

The larder door was ajar and banging every time the gusts came through the small window. I closed both, and returned through the roaring to my bed.

But sleep was impossible. We get these frighteningly strong winds up here on the downs, and a great deal of damage is done to our houses and farm buildings, not to mention trees and gardens. Usually I comfort myself with the thought that I have survived plenty of these rough nights, but this one seemed peculiarly vicious. One thing, it would test Reg Thorn's new window, I thought.

I dropped off again about six, the storm still raging, so that I overslept and had to hurry around to get over to school in time. To my dismay there was rain water on the floor beneath the window. On looking up, I could see that the whole structure seemed to be slanting, but that the water appeared to be dripping to the right of it.

I went outside and bumped into Mr Willet, and pointed out the damage. He surveyed it in silence for a full minute.

'It's the roof timbers, I reckon, not so much the window. It's no good patching old with new and expecting 'em both to thrive. Best get old Reg again, I suppose.'

He came inside with me and surveyed the puddle. Drips from above enlarged it steadily.

'Quite like old times, ain't it?' said Mr Willet, with evident satisfaction.

I rang Reg and left a message with his wife as he was out, of course. Mrs Pringle was mopping up when I returned. She was wearing a new cretonne overall and an expression of extreme martyrdom.

'This is something I could have done without,' she said sourly. 'My leg's proper blazing this morning. I didn't hardly know how to get up the street.'

'I'll get one of the children to do it,' I said. Mrs Pringle wrung out the floor cloth, and shuffled to her feet.

'Too late! It's done now. And I hope you'll tell Reg Thorn what you think of him when he deigns to turn up.'

I told her that I had telephoned.

'Well, I shall have a word with him whatever you decide to do. Shoddy workmanship, that's what that is.'

'What a pretty overall,' I replied, trying to pour oil on troubled waters. The old harridan looked slightly less gloomy.

'Minnie give it to me when she left. That's one blessing, I must say, to have the house to myself at last. But for how long, I wonder? That girl's still hankering after that Bert, you know. It's as though she can't help herself. Nothing but a prawn of fate, if you take my meaning.'

I said that I thought I did.

'Well, Ern's come round, and seems to be working regular – if work you can call it, leaning on a spade up Springbourne Manor and having cups of tea at all hours in the greenhouse. He don't know yet about Bert, and I've threatened to tell him, to try and get our Min to come to her senses. Sometimes I wonder if she's right in her head, Miss Read, I do straight.'

I agreed warmly. Mrs Pringle picked up her pail and limped to the lobby.

Later, Miss Briggs and I surveyed the damaged window more closely, as we awaited the arrival of Reg Thorn.

'It seems such a shame after all that hard work,' said my assistant.

'It does. By the way, did you know that the dark young man's name was Richards?'

'Yes.'

'Reg Thorn tells me that his father has had a stroke, poor fellow.'

'I know.'

'I wonder if it means that Wayne will have to leave Reg Thorn? He seemed to think so. It is bad luck.'

'Not for Wayne, I shouldn't think,' observed Miss Briggs, and the conversation ended abruptly as the youngest Coggs child approached bearing a dead, and very smelly, starling.

Afterwards it occurred to me that Miss Briggs seemed to

know far more about the Richards than I did. Hardly surprising, I told myself, as she talked to the two boys far more than I did, and may well have bumped into them in Caxley recently.

Reg Thorn did not arrive until school ended. It was still blowing, still cold, and still depressing. I went indoors for my tea, leaving him to discover the worst. Twenty minutes later, having thawed out, I repented, and took him out a mug of tea.

But he had gone.

Rehearsals continued, and I was glad to see that the children seemed much less self-conscious as they began to be familiar with their lines and their movements about the stage – or rather, the schoolroom floor.

The costumes were practically finished, thanks largely I knew to Mrs Moffat's generosity with her time and skill. Nothing second-rate ever came from that lady's needle, and I was confident that our cast would be beautifully dressed.

We ran through the whole programme to time it one afternoon, and were pleasantly surprised to find that the whole thing took about an hour and a quarter. As we were following this with our tea party, we should have two full and happy afternoons, the first for the infants' parents and friends, and the repeat performance the next day for the juniors and the rest of those wanting to come.

The vicar called in one day to give me the good news that the managers were providing our birthday cake, and that Mrs Willet had offered to bake it – or rather two of them, one for each afternoon.

'It's very generous of them,' I said. 'And if Mrs Willet's in charge of the cooking, we know everything will be absolutely superb.'

'It was Henry's idea really. He thought Mrs Willet, as an

old Fairacre pupil, might be agreeable, and she just jumped at the chance. She said it would have been a disgrace to ask some Caxley baker to make Fairacre's centenary cake. She's working out the cost, which we're delighted to meet as our small contribution to the fun.'

It was marvellous to see how enthusiastic the whole village was about our celebrations. There was no doubt about it, Fairacre School was the heart of our village, and memories of their own schooldays quickened the adults' response to this tribute to its hundred years. Its influence could never be estimated. I only hoped that it would be able to continue to serve the village as it had always done.

Our numbers were smaller than ever before, and I did my best to push that unpleasant fact, and its even more unpleasant consequences, into the back of my mind.

But I was not always successful.

Joan Benson rang one evening to invite me to a small party for farewell drinks.

'I'd love to come,' I said, 'but "farewell" sounds so sad.'

'Oh, I think I shall pop back from time to time,' she said cheerfully. 'Miriam insists, and so do Irene and David. I must say that now it's arrived, I feel much happier about going than I have all these months.'

'So you've found something in Sussex?'

'I think so. Nothing really fixed yet, but David and Irene have sold their flat, and their buyers want to move in almost immediately. The Mawnes were very sweet and did not want to hurry me – in fact they'd made plans to stay in Caxley, or with Henry and Elizabeth – but it's far better for everyone if they move in here at once, and in any case, I can stay with my daughter until my new abode is ready.'

'We shall all miss you. Particularly Miriam.'

'It's kind of you to say so. Actually Miriam seems much more settled about the move now. I think she's suddenly realized that the Mawnes genuinely want her to stay, and now that she feels she can be useful to them, her attitude has changed entirely. I must say, I feel much happier about deserting her. She so loves Fairacre, it would have been tragic if she had had to uproot herself after such a short stay.'

I wished her luck with her plans, and said that I would look forward to the party on December the first.

Two days later Reg Thorn arrived with three men who, from their somewhat formal attire, were probably from the building department of the county education office. They all gazed at the poor dormer window, still hopelessly askew, and a good deal of head-shaking went on and grave looks were exchanged. From my strategic lookout post by the classroom window it seemed that Reg Thorn grew increasingly unhappy during the conference, but of course I could not hear what was being said.

After about half an hour, when we had settled down to arithmetic, one of the three strangers knocked at the door and asked if he could have a word with me. Reg Thorn and the other two men seemed to have disappeared.

'I'm afraid that this is going to be a bigger job than we thought,' he said. 'Mr Thorn will be dismantling the present structure immediately, as it is not too safe.'

I must have looked alarmed, for he went on hastily.

'Nothing too daunting! You and the children will be quite all right. But for the time being we propose to put a large piece of perspex over the aperture to keep out the weather while we investigate the roof timbers again.'

Trust our Mr Willet to have been right from the word 'Go', was my private comment, but naturally I kept mum.

'And when will Reg Thorn start the dismantling?' I asked.

'This afternoon,' replied the man. He sounded rather grim, I thought. 'And the sooner the better,' he added.

I was in entire agreement.

Mrs Willet called in during the evening to return a cookery book which I had lent her some time ago, and I took the opportunity of saying how pleased we all were to hear that she was making the birthday cake.

'*Cakes*,' she corrected me. 'It wouldn't be seemly to have half a cake at the second tea party. It's just as simple to make two nice cakes as the one.' She hesitated for a moment. 'Which brings me to the candles,' she continued.

'How do you mean?'

'Well, I reckon we ought to have a hundred candles – those weeny little cake ones, you know – and now I'll need *two* hundred for the two cakes.'

It seemed what her husband would call 'a mort of candles' to me, but I supposed she knew best.

'I've got it all planned out, you see. I'm doing two big square cakes, because it's easier to cut them fairly that way. And if I put ten candles to a row, and have ten rows, it will work out lovely.'

I expressed genuine admiration.

'Oh, it's nothing,' said Mrs Willet modestly. 'I've been baking big cakes in Fairacre for all my married life – W.I. dos and Sunday School treats and that, but I want these two cakes to be the best I've ever done – a sort of "Thank you" to the school. Anyway, I enjoy a good baking day.'

'I bet Mr Willet does too,' I said.

'Oh, he's a splendid eater!' said his wife enthusiastically. 'Always was. We always said the Willet boys had enough in their dinner basket to feed the whole school.'

I remembered Mr Willet's remark about his recently dead brother who had carried the rush basket to school, and the largesse from Grandma which topped up the original victuals.

'I remember Miss Clare saying once that as long as a person could eat, then there couldn't be much wrong with him. She used to give us lessons about hygiene as we got to the top of the school. Very useful too in later life. Sometimes I used to think poor Mr Hope might not have taken to drink if he had had a better appetite. Hardly ate anything, you know. Mrs Hope used to worry about it. But there, he was a poet, poor soul, as no doubt you know, Miss Read, and poets don't seem to need food, do they?'

I thought of Timothy Ferdinand wolfing down Amy's delicious provender at her dinner party, and asking for the veal patties to take home.

'Some don't, I imagine, Mrs Willet,' I said diplomatically, 'but there are undoubtedly some poets who do.'

'Maybe, but what I was going to ask you, Miss Read, was could you possibly buy the candles for me when you go to Caxley on Saturday? I'd like to have them in good time, and I've no plans to go into town just yet.'

I said I would be very pleased to do it.

'And you will get a receipt, won't you?' she begged. 'The managers want to pay every penny, and have told me to make a note of *everything*.'

I promised that I would do so, and she departed looking relieved.

The job of dismantling the offending dormer window went along at a spanking pace. I thought ruefully that it was obviously much quicker to demolish than to build, remembering the months we had endured noise and the ingress of the weather.

To my surprise, Wayne Richards reappeared as well as his former companion. I asked after his father.

'Getting on fine, that's why I'm here for the rest of the week. Reg is in a bit of a taking over this business, and Dad said it would be best to help him out, as the job's got to be done quickly.'

I did not like to ask about his own plans for the future, but he volunteered the information.

'I'm starting in with Dad on a business footing at the beginning of December. Suits us both very well, and there's plenty of work about. He's not one to get in a panic about his health, but I think this last attack rocked him, and he won't do as much as he always has done. About time he eased off a bit, and I'll be glad to take over more of the work. There's only me to carry it on, so I'd better learn the ropes pretty quickly.'

He gave me a flashing smile through the black beard, and mounted the ladder again.

Amy arrived one afternoon in the same week just as the children were going home. She had asked me to look through the article about the sick room and to give her my opinion on it.

The two young men were up on the roof manhandling the large piece of perspex into place.

'Shan't see you tomorrow,' shouted Wayne. 'We'll have this fixed tonight in case we get some rain.'

'Well, thanks for all you've done,' I called back.

Amy and I walked across the playground to my house where Tibby, ever ravenous, gave us a rapturous welcome.

'What's his name?' enquired Amy, slipping off her coat.

'Who?'

'The bearded fellow. Miss Briggs's young man.'

'Miss Briggs's young man?' I echoed. 'That's Reg Thorn's young man! He's called Wayne Richards. His father's a builder too.'

'He's also Miss Briggs's young man,' said Amy

patiently. 'At least, he's the one she was with way back in the summer. The one I told you about.'

'You didn't tell me it was *Wayne*,' I said accusingly.

'I didn't know it was Wayne until two seconds ago,' said Amy reasonably. 'But that's certainly the same fellow. I couldn't forget a beard of that magnitude.'

'Well, I'm blowed!' I said, turning over this interesting piece of knowledge. 'I had no idea this was going on, but it explains quite a lot.'

'How do you mean?'

'Well, the improvement in temper, and the willingness to stay after school – at least, until the boy finishes work. I wonder I didn't twig before, with all this happening before my very eyes, as they say.'

'Why should you? They weren't likely to be particularly demonstrative before you and all those knowing pupils. As two sensible young people they hoped to keep their affairs to themselves, as far as you can in a village.'

'Well, I must say I'm delighted with the news. He's a good fellow, and going to have a steady job with his father. I would have thought he could have done better than our Miss Briggs, though.'

'No doubt she has hidden charms,' said Amy.

'Obviously.' I continued to think about this interesting disclosure.

'One thing,' I told Amy. 'She'll probably stay here teaching. It will be nice to know that I shan't have to start advertising for another infants' teacher yet.'

'Aren't you rushing ahead a trifle?' enquired Amy. 'Give the poor things time to sort out their romance.'

'Who started all this anyway?' I retorted.

12. December

Our temporary skylight was a great success. For one thing, it was considerably wider than the original one, as the aperture had been made larger to take the ill-fated dormer window, and so allowed much more light to come through.

As it lay snug and flat against the roof there was no dreadful drumming noise, and from outside, I must say, the line of the roof looked better to my eyes than the somewhat clumsy dormer window. I was beginning to wonder if the powers that be would finally decide to replace the old skylight with another of more up-to-date construction.

The men who had come with Reg Thorn to inspect the damage after the gale, came again after school one day and spent a long session inside and outside the old building.

Their decision was conveyed to me later by a letter from the office telling me that work on the roof timbers would be put in hand as soon as school broke up. The new window would be finished before the children returned in January, and they were sorry for the inconvenience. They added, rather decently I thought, that unusually severe weather had jeopardized Mr Thorn's work, and that further consultations would be needed to settle the design of the new lights, under the circumstances.

'Mark my words,' said Mr Willet, when I mentioned this to him. 'Reg Thorn will be putting in another skylight. And a durn good thing too. That dormer was wrong from the start, for our old roof. I told you, didn't I, they must have gone into all that pretty thorough when the old place was built in 1880? And they built to last then too.'

Mrs Pringle, who had entered during this conversation, added her mite.

'One thing, it should make Reg Thorn get a move on for once. I take it he won't get paid till the job's done, and he must have lost a packet already. It's an ill wind as blows nobody any good.'

Joan Benson's sitting room was crowded when I arrived on the evening of the party.

It was a pleasant surprise to see David and Irene Mawne among the guests, and Joan was busy introducing the new owners of Holly Lodge to the one or two other people whom they had not met before. Irene's brother, Horace Umbleditch, who teaches at a prep school not far from Amy at Bent, was also there, and it was good to see him again.

The room was looking very festive with a ceiling-high Christmas tree already in place.

'Too early, I know,' said Joan, to the admirers, 'but I intended to enjoy my last Christmas here, and to have all the trimmings.'

I found myself by Henry Mawne and asked when his nephew hoped to move in.

'Just before Christmas, I think, though one can never be certain of these things. The removal people seem to think about the 20th December, and Joan has been absolutely adamant that she will be out by then. We are full of admiration for the way she is coping. She's definitely having the house she went to see a week or so ago, and luckily, those people are off on the twelfth.'

'Can she be sure?'

'He's in the army and being posted to the Middle East. That's one thing about the services, once you've got your marching orders, you know where you are. A great relief all round. David's buyers fiddled about until he and Irene were nearly demented, but now that's satisfactorily tied up.'

Miriam Quinn approached and Henry drifted away to talk to the vicar. I asked her if she were going away for Christmas.

'Yes, I'm off to Norfolk to my brother's. I thought it would be more fun for David and Irene to have their first Christmas here on their own. Of course, young Simon will be here, and I believe Henry and Elizabeth have been invited to Christmas dinner. Quite a family affair, and I shall enjoy being with my own folk too, of course. What are you going to do?'

I told her that I had in mind to invite Dolly Clare to spend Christmas and Boxing Day with me. She would be with me overnight for the centenary celebrations earlier in the month, but if she were willing to come later as well, it would be an added joy.

'Do you know, I've never met her, and would love to.'

'Then we'll fix up a meeting in the New Year,' I promised. 'But we're being called to order.'

Sure enough, the vicar called for silence, and made a graceful little speech, wishing Joan well and welcoming the young Mawnes. We raised our glasses, and drank their healths.

I thought, yet again, how lucky we are in Fairacre to have so many good people united in friendship within our parish bounds.

As our two-day celebrations drew near, excitement began to run high. As well as the entertainment, it was my duty, as always, to provide the annual village tea party. This is paid for from our school funds, raised during the year by such things as jumble sales and bazaars, and I do the ordering.

This time it was obvious that we should need twice as much food, although Mrs Willet's masterpieces should certainly fill up appreciative stomachs. We are lucky enough still to have a baker in Fairacre. He also keeps the village shop, so that I went up one evening to discuss with him such things as scones, buns, lardy cake, and what he calls 'confections' – that is such mouth-watering and fattening things as almond slices, macaroons and madeleines.

Usually I order sliced loaves as well, and spend hours making sandwiches in my kitchen. But this year, with so much else to occupy my time, I decided to give them a miss.

By the time we had finished poring over the order, it was plain to me that we should have to have some more money-raising efforts early in the New Year, as the existing school kitty would be seriously depleted.

And why not, I asked myself? It's not every year that one celebrates one's hundredth birthday! Fairacre School was going to do its friends proud – and enjoy every minute of it.

The two performances and tea parties were to take place on the last Thursday and Friday of term.

Mrs Annett from Beech Green (who as Miss Gray was once my infants' teacher until the neighbouring head-master snatched her from me into matrimony) brought Miss Clare with her, as our old friend was to stay the night so that she did not get over-tired. I was to return her to her own cottage on Friday evening.

At half-past two parents and friends came flooding into the ancient schoolroom. We had pushed back the dividing partition, and the action was to take place at the infants'

end of the room. The quaking actors and actresses were
huddled into the lobby. Miss Clare, serene as ever, did her
best to calm their nerves while I greeted our guests, and
told them a little of what they would be seeing – with
reasonable luck.

I had never seen our little school so packed, and this, of
course, was only half our audience. I found it intensely
moving to see so many old people, some of whom had been
pupils before the First World War and would remember
Miss Clare as a young pupil teacher. It was good too to see
so many friends, some comparative newcomers to
Fairacre, like the Mawnes, who had come to do us honour
and to join in this home-spun tribute to our school.

I read the entry from the original log book, and Linda
and Patrick took the stage. There was warm applause as
they entered, due largely, I think, to the superb costumes
which Mrs Moffat had created.

After looking somewhat scared at this unexpected welcome, the two became quite confident, and went through
their little scene. The caning went down extremely well,
and a baby in the front row brought the house down by
shouting: 'Give 'im some more!' in the most bloodthirsty
manner. Obviously, I should have to keep an eye on this
juvenile sadist when he came under my care in two or three
years' time.

'In King Edward the Seventh's reign,' I said loudly, for
hidden Dolly Clare's benefit, 'Fairacre School had a new
young pupil teacher.'

Here Dolly entered, smiling, and the applause grew
deafening. We had placed the old high chair, in which she
had sat for so many years, in front of the audience, and
with just one page of notes Dolly began her reminiscences.

Her listeners gave her rapt attention. She confined her
memories to the early years of her teaching at the school,
and mentioned many children – many now dead, or killed

in the 1914–18 war – remembered clearly by the older ones present.

She touched on the clothes worn, the lunches brought, the great distances trudged in all weathers, and the universal poverty which dogged almost all. She also dwelt on the happiness found in simple things: the occasional treat, the annual outing, harvest home, a visit from the bishop, as well as the ineffable joy of country things such as the first primroses, the cuckoo's call and the return of the .swallows.

There was no doubt about it. As I had suspected, Miss Clare's contribution, made incidentally without any recourse to her notes, was the highlight of the afternoon, although the following scene, showing the school's part in the war of George the Fifth's reign, obviously moved many of those who could remember those sad times.

Mr Lamb's recollections of the trip to Wembley from the school gave us all a chance to laugh. Some of his contemporaries interrupted his narrative with downright contradictions, but it was all done with such enthusiasm and merriment that his contribution was a resounding success.

Mrs Austen's vivid account of an evacuee's view of Fairacre was warmly received, and probably because she was a woman, she was not open to the same outspoken comments which had punctuated Mr Lamb's account.

Then it was my turn to give an idea of the school in the reign of our present Queen Elizabeth the Second. I had tried to make it a brief survey and as interesting as possible, but feared it might be something of a comedown after the earlier contributions.

It was a kind audience, however, and genuinely interested, I felt, in the changes which had taken place since the Act of 1944 when the children over eleven went off to Beech Green or Caxley Grammar School, and Fairacre was left as a junior school. The repercussions of the ancient

grammar school being obliged to become a comprehensive school were also mentioned, for this fact touched many of the families present.

The children's work was on display round the walls and at one end of the room, and I invited the audience to inspect everything and to see how methods of work had altered over the hundred years. The whole school then clustered on to our temporary stage and sang two songs very sweetly.

Finally, the vicar rose and made a fine speech about the great part this old school had played in village life, and complimented everyone on the work done, not only on the stage this afternoon, but behind the scenes for many, many years. He then asked us all to join in a prayer of thanksgiving for mercies received in the past, and to call a blessing on Fairacre School's future.

While this was being done and heads were bent, I could hear the welcome sound of Mrs Pringle and her band of helpers, dealing with the tea things in the other lobby. Festivity was about to follow reverence.

It was astonishing to see how quickly the mounds of provender vanished. Appetites are keen in our sharp downland air, and I was kept busy filling cups from the tea urn borrowed from the Woman's Institute for the two occasions.

But at last the great moment came when the vicar called for silence, the door opened and Mrs Willet came staggering in, bearing the magnificent cake ablaze with one hundred candles. A great cheer went up and the ancient floorboards quaked under the stamping of stout country boots.

We had asked Miss Clare, as the oldest pupil present, and the youngest child from the infants' room to cut the cake together. My bread knife only just proved equal to severing the beautifully dark, rich mixture, but the two won through eventually and a slice was delivered to everyone present.

It was dark by the time the last of our visitors had gone. The fragrance of the fruit cake still lingered about the empty schoolroom, and far too many crumbs lay upon the floor.

'It all went beautifully,' I said to Miss Clare before we walked across the playground to my home. 'But I don't know what Mrs Pringle will say when she sees the mess.'

'What Mrs Pringle says,' Miss Clare told me, 'can have very little meaning in face of a hundred years of our school's history.'

And with this comforting thought we strolled home to take our ease. There was a sharp nip in the air, and our breath was visible in the dusk.

'A frost tonight,' said Miss Clare. 'The first real one of the winter.'

Sure enough, when I took her breakfast tray into my spare room the next morning, the trees and grass were white with hoar frost. It was a lovely sight, but a pointer to things to come.

Miss Clare protested about being waited on, but I was adamant that she stayed in bed for an hour or two longer. We had a repeat performance to go through in the afternoon, and I knew that there would be a great many friends who would want to talk to her.

As it was the last day of term, too, I should be busy clearing up and trying to remind the children of the date of our return in January, as well as keeping them relatively calm and prepared for their final performance. I found that it was no easy task. Success had quite gone to their heads, and I had never known them quite so excited and noisy. I pushed them out early to play in the frosty playground and to run off some of their excess energy.

Miss Briggs, whose class was suffering from the same *joie de vivre*, joined me in the playground, and we gave them all a further ten minutes of strenuous exercise. If anything, these tactics seemed to rouse them even more, but we ushered the breathless mob indoors, and I suggested that a story might calm them down.

'We have to expect this sort of thing on the last day of term,' I said indulgently. 'And then, of course, there's Christmas looming ahead. Are you going home?'

'Yes,' said my assistant.

'Tonight? Will you want to get off early?'

I wished I could remember if it were Droitwich or Harrogate. Somewhere a good distance away, I knew.

'No. It seemed better to go tomorrow in the light, and anyway Wayne doesn't finish until tomorrow morning.'

I must have looked blank.

'I'm driving home to Leamington and taking him with me.'

Leamington. I must remember *Leamington.*

'That will be nice for you both,' I said, anxious not to appear too pressing, but Miss Briggs was well launched.

'My parents know about him, of course, but haven't met him yet. I expect we'll announce our engagement at Christmas.'

I said, quite truthfully, that I was delighted to hear the news, and that Wayne was a fine young man.

Miss Briggs gave me the biggest smile I had yet seen upon her countenance, and we returned to the noisy rabble within.

Our second afternoon was even more successful than the first. For one thing, all those taking part were more relaxed, and the audience was even larger than the day before. How they all managed to squeeze in I shall never fathom.

Mrs Willet's second cake was as rapturously received as the first, and almost all the school's offerings went too. The few cakes that remained, I put into a paper bag to give surreptitiously to the Coggs family later.

Miss Clare was surrounded by friends, among them Elizabeth Mawne who had not met her before. Their conversation was animated, and I was glad to see my old friend Dolly so lively. I began to realize, more sharply than ever before, that she normally lacked company, and I was glad that I was about to invite her to spend Christmas with me.

Even Mrs Pringle seemed to have mellowed with our festivities, and said nothing about the floor strewn with crumbs.

'I'll see to that tea urn,' she said. 'The W.I. can turn a bit funny if it's not returned pronto, and *clean.*'

At last we said goodbye to our guests, reiterated the phrase: 'Term begins on January the sixth' to those willing to listen, who were few among the general pandemonium, and left the schoolroom to the ministrations of Mrs Pringle and Mr and Mrs Willet, who insisted on putting all to rights.

'Well,' I said to Miss Clare, when we sank exhausted one each side of my sitting-room fire. 'I'm whacked! Someone else will have to cope with the next centenary.'

'But it's really been *memorable*!' replied Dolly. 'How glad I am to have seen it – and to have taken part!'

'Have a glass of sherry,' I said, struggling to my feet. 'We need a pick-me-up after all that.'

'Here's to Fairacre School,' said Dolly, raising her glass, and we drank thankfully.

'Have you any plans for Christmas?' I asked, after the first rejuvenating mouthful.

'None. Except that I expect the kind Annetts will invite me there for Christmas Day.'

I said how much I should like her to come to Fairacre for the two days, or longer if she could manage it.

'There's nothing I should enjoy more,' she told me. And so it was happily settled.

'I can honestly say I never feel truly lonely,' she went on, 'but now that I'm such a great age I've no one of my own left. Ada's children lost touch years ago, even before my sister died. Of course, dear Emily meant more to me than anyone in the world, but when she went there was really no one left, except good friends like you. I believe you are in the same boat?'

'I suppose so. No really close relations, though I have a dear aunt, and some jolly cousins, but they are all as busy as I am, and we don't keep in touch as we should. No, I'm like you, very glad of good friends who live near enough to see frequently, like you and the Annetts and dear old Amy at Bent, who wants to meet you incidentally.'

'That will be nice,' said Dolly. She sounded a trifle abstracted, and I wondered if she were over-tired, which would not be surprising. She took another sip from her glass, and then put it carefully on the side table.

'I think I ought to tell you something which perhaps I should have told you before. When I was talking to that nice Mrs Mawne this afternoon, I realized for the first time that you might be worrying about what might happen to you if this school ever had to close.'

'Well, that's been a possibility for years, of course,' I said, puzzled.

'You see, my dear, having no relatives to speak of, I left everything to dear Emily as she had nowhere of her own to live, and only a tiny pension. Not that I had much more, of course, but I did have the cottage to shelter us. When she had gone, I went one day to Caxley to see young Mr Lovejoy and to alter my will.'

Young Mr Lovejoy, I knew, was about to retire as he

was now in his sixties. But to Miss Clare, whose family had dealt with the old-established solicitors for two or three generations, young Mr Lovejoy must seem a mere boy.

'He was as charming as ever,' said Dolly, 'and we made out a nice simple little will, leaving some money to the church at Beech Green and the same to Fairacre. My few trinkets I've left to Isobel Annett. Nothing much of value there, I'm afraid, but some are quite pretty.'

'She'll treasure them, I'm sure,' I said.

Miss Clare picked up her glass again. 'And the house I've left to you.'

I felt my jaw drop. I gazed at her, speechless with shock.

'Do you mind?' asked Dolly very gently.

'Mind?' I croaked. 'I don't know what to say!'

'I wanted it to be a surprise for you when I'd gone. I knew you hadn't made any arrangements to buy a place, and I thought you could find a home there while you looked round, if you wanted something better.'

'There is nothing better!' I whispered. My voice seemed to have collapsed completely, and my heart was jumping about like a frog.

'Well, of course, I'd always hoped that you would want to live in it, and be as happy as I have there. I ought to have realized though that you might be worrying about the future. It wasn't until this afternoon, when Mrs Mawne mentioned it, that I saw that I had really been rather self-indulgent in trying to keep my plans secret.'

'Dolly,' I began, trying to control my wavering voice, 'I don't know how to thank you. I'm absolutely overwhelmed, and don't deserve such generosity. I'll try to tell you soon how I feel – but I'm too overjoyed for words just now.'

'Good!' said Dolly comfortably. 'Well, that's settled. Now to more practical matters. What would you like for a Christmas present?'

I went over to kiss her.

'You've just given me one,' I told her.

Later that evening, I took Dolly home, and saw her safely into bed with her hot water bottle and a warm drink. By that time, I had recovered enough to tell her how I felt about her wonderful gesture. It made the future quite different for me, and I was still too dazed to comprehend fully just what it would mean.

I locked the cottage door as directed, and put the key back through the letter box. I still could not believe that one day – long distant, I sincerely prayed – this lovely house might be mine.

'I shall never sleep a wink,' I said to myself, as I drove back through the frosty night.

But I fell into bed within ten minutes of reaching home, and slept like a log until seven.

I resolved to say nothing about my proposed legacy to any one. Dolly wanted to keep it a secret, and I should respect that wish.

But buoyed up with my wonderful news, I set about all the Christmas tasks I had neglected during our celebrations.

Christmas cards were arriving thick and fast. Trees, flowers, robins, skating parties, and every imaginable winter activity glowed from the tributes on my mantelpiece, and I must get down to sending off some of my own.

The card I cherished most was a photograph of a baby seal sent to me by the kind people at the Tresco hotel. The seal had been born on the beach nearby, and no other Christmas card could touch it for its delightful appeal. It took pride of place among the others.

It also galvanized me into doing something which Amy had urged me to do long ago. The first letter of the holidays was to that same hotel, booking a room for a fortnight in August. How Amy would approve!

The frost continued. The ground was iron hard and every morning found the grass and trees covered with hoar frost. Ice was everywhere, and the roads treacherous.

Miss Clare sent a message to say that she had decided against coming to the school service at St Patrick's the next Sunday, because of the weather, but would look forward to seeing me on Christmas Eve for tea at her house. We should miss her at the service, but I was relieved to know that she was not venturing out in this bitter weather. I hoped that by the following Wednesday the thaw would have set in.

Attendance at morning service on Sunday must have delighted Gerald Partridge's heart. Parents, pupils, managers and other friends of Fairacre School turned up in full force, and there were very few empty pews.

The singing was hearty, and I had found time to coach the children in the two hymns chosen particularly for this occasion, so that they added to the joyful noise considerably. The vicar's sermon was a model of sincerity, brevity and gratitude, and Mr Annett had chosen some stirring music for the service. The final voluntary was Mozart's 'Turkish March', and I wondered, yet again, how anyone, Turks or otherwise, could march in step to that dancing rhythm.

But it was a joyous and uplifting ending to our centenary celebrations.

By Wednesday, the murky cold weather had lifted slightly. It was still bitterly cold, but the roads had thawed, and for two or three hours at midday a feeble sun dispersed the clouds.

I drove over to Beech Green and walked up the short path to Dolly Clare's cottage with the most unusual feelings. Pleasure at being there was now mingled with something like awe. That this, one day, might be mine! I could still not fully realize my good fortune, and felt very humble in the face of Dolly's superb generosity. Of one thing I could be certain. The cottage would be cherished as dearly as before, and if ever her gentle ghost reappeared it would be given honour and a warm welcome.

We were at St Patrick's the next morning, admiring the Christmas roses, the holly, the ivy and the mistletoe. Mr Partridge's suggestion that the children might help had not been followed up, and certainly the flower-arranging ladies had made a superb job of their labour of love without juvenile aid.

We walked back through the thin winter sunshine to find that the chicken I had left roasting was done to a turn, and the small pudding was bubbling cheerfully on the stove.

After our modest Christmas dinner we indulged in a glass of port and both slipped off into slumber, awaking just in time to listen to the Queen's message.

We spent the rest of Christmas Day and Boxing Day very quietly and lazily, going for short walks round the familiar lanes of Fairacre when the sun came through in the early afternoon. But it was always good to return to the fireside and to pick up our knitting, or attempt to solve the crossword puzzle, or sometimes simply to doze. To tell the truth, I was dog-tired at the end of term, and this one had been particularly arduous. Not that I would have missed any of our jollifications for a minute, but I began to realize just how exhausted I was when I could relax at home. Dolly Clare was the perfect companion for this pace of life, serene, undemanding and unfailingly happy.

I managed to persuade her to stay until the Saturday morning, but no longer. She was anxious not to put her good neighbour to any unnecessary trouble.

'She is looking after the cat,' she said, 'and getting in my milk and bread. And no doubt she will light a fire, and generally cosset the house, so I must get back to look after it myself.'

We drove over in the morning, and sure enough a fire blazed in the grate. We settled down to enjoy a cup of coffee before I returned.

'I've lived here for six reigns now,' said Miss Clare, looking about her. 'I thought when I was telling our friends about my time as a pupil teacher at Fairacre, that I must have closed the door of this cottage some thousands of times and set off on my bicycle along the lane to that dear old school. I've seen the trees and fields breaking into leaf, shading the road later, turning into the gold of autumn and then bitter nakedness, for more years than I care to remember. But always this cottage has been the beginning and end of every journey. The thought that you will do the same after me gives me infinite pleasure. I don't know when I've felt quite so happy.'

'I can echo that,' I told her.

No snow came to our downland country during the remaining days of December, but the skies were ominously grey and the iron cold made one feel that this respite might be short-lived. On New Year's Eve I was invited to the Mawnes for the evening. I walked through the village in the frosty air to the sound of the bells ringing a practice peal at St Patrick's.

Well, the Old Year had been good to me, I thought. I had seen Fairacre School celebrating a hundred years of useful work, and my personal life had been enriched by friends old and new. And Dolly Clare's incredible kindness had put the final seal upon a memorable year. I had a great deal to be thankful for.

So what would the New Year bring, I wondered,

opening the gate of the Mawnes's house? Lights gleamed in the windows. A lantern by the door lit up the welcoming holly wreath dangling its scarlet ribbons against the white paint.

'Come in, come in!' called Henry, opening the door, 'and a Happy New Year to you, and all Fairacre!'

MORE ABOUT PENGUINS, PELICANS
AND PUFFINS

For further information about books available from Penguins please write to Dept EP, Penguin Books Ltd, Harmondsworth, Middlesex UB7 ODA.

In the U.S.A.: For a complete list of books available from Penguins in the United States write to Dept DG, Penguin Books, 299 Murray Hill Parkway, East Rutherford, New Jersey 07073.

In Canada: For a complete list of books available from Penguins in Canada write to Penguin Books Canada Ltd, 2801 John Street Markham, Ontario L3R 1B4.

In Australia: For a complete list of books available from Penguins in Australia write to the Marketing Department, Penguin Books Australia Ltd, P.O. Box 257, Ringwood, Victoria 3134.

In New Zealand: For a complete list of books available from Penguins in New Zealand write to the Marketing Department, Penguin Books (N.Z.) Ltd, P.O. Box 4019, Auckland 10.

In India: For a complete list of books available from Penguins in India write to Penguin Overseas Ltd, 706 Eros Apartments, 56 Nehru Place, New Delhi 110019.